Maybe the hardest thing about moving overseas was being in a place where no one but your own family had any memory of you. It was like putting yourself back together with little pieces.

At home in St. Louis even the man at the grocery store remembered the day a very young Liyana poked a ripe peach too hard and her finger went inside it. She shrieked and the neighborhood ladies buying vegetables laughed. Forever after when she came into his store the grocer would say "Be careful with my plums! Don't get too close to my melons!"

It was a little thing, of course, but it helped her to be *somebody*.

In Jerusalem she was just a blur going by on the streets. The half-American with Arab eyes in the blue Armenian school uniform.

Who?

Critical acclaim for *Habibi*

"Readers will be engaged by the character, the romance, the foreshadowed danger. Poetically imaged and leavened with humor, the story renders layered and complex history understandable through character and incident. *Habibi* succeeds in making the hope for peace compelling, personal and concrete."—*School Library Journal*

"[B]reaks new ground in YA fiction."
—Hazel Rochman, *Booklist*

"This is the work of a poet, not a polemicist. The very title, an Arabic form of endearment that has been adopted into everyday Hebrew, bespeaks a vision of a gentler world in which kisses are more common than gunshots."
—*Houston Chronicle*

"Nye's prose keeps both feet on the ground, barefoot, while her eyes are fixed on the angels."—*Aramco World*

ALA Best Book for Young Adults
ALA Notable Children's Book
Jane Addams Book Award
New York Public Library Book for the Teen Age
American Bookseller "Pick of the Lists"
Judy Lopez Memorial Award for Children's Literature
Texas Institute of Letters Best Book
for Young Readers

HABIBI

— ◆ —

Naomi Shihab Nye

SIMON PULSE

First paperback edition June 1999
Copyright © 1997 by Naomi Shihab Nye

Simon Pulse
An imprint of Simon & Schuster
Children's Publishing Division
1230 Avenue of the Americas
New York, NY 10020

Also available in a Simon & Schuster Books for Young Readers
hardcover edition.
Book design by Heather Wood.
The text of this book is set in American Garamond.

Printed and bound in the United States of America

20 19 18 17 16 15 14 13 12

The Library of Congress has cataloged the hardcover edition as follows:
Nye, Naomi Shihab

Habibi: a novel / by Naomi Shihab Nye

p. cm.

Summary: When fourteen-year-old Liyana Abboud, her younger brother, and her parents move from St. Louis to a new home between Jerusalem and the Palestinian village where her father was born, they face many changes and must deal with the tensions between Jews and Palestinians.
ISBN 0-689-80149-1 (hc.)
[1. Family life—Jerusalem—Fiction. 2. Jerusalem—Fiction.
3. Emigration and immigration—Fiction. 4. Jewish—Arab relations—Fiction.]
I. Title. PZ7.N976Hab 1997 [Fic]—dc21 97-10943 CIP AC
ISBN 0-689-82523-4 (pbk.)

"Damascus Gate" by Yehuda Amichai appears in *Selected Poetry of Yehuda Amichai*, Translated by Chana Bloch and Stephen Mitchell
(Harper & Row, 1986)

"Homing Pigeons" by Mahmoud Darwish was translated by Lena Jayyusi and W.S. Merwin and appears in *Anthology of Modern Palestinian Literature*, Edited by Salma Khadra Jayyusi (Columbia University Press, 1992)

Thanks to Kevin Henkes and Andrea Carlisle for their friendship and advice, to Madison Nye for his technological expertise, to Anton Shammas for his inspiration, to Madhatters Tea, San Antonio, to Sarah Thomson and Susan Rich, and especially to my editor, Virginia Duncan, who knows both when to drink Vietnamese iced coffee and when to crack the whip.

For my father, Aziz
and my mother, Miriam
who have loved us so well

For Adlai, my brother

For Grace and Hillary Nye

For my Armenian friends in the Old City of Jerusalem

And for all the Arabs and Jews
who would rather be cousins than enemies

For you

Habibi

I forget how this street looked
a month ago, but I can remember it,
say, from the Time of the Crusades.

(Pardon me, you dropped this. Is it yours?
This stone? Not *that* one, that one fell
nine hundred years ago.)

From "Damascus Gate," by Yehuda Amichai

Where do you take me, my love, away from my
    parents
from my trees, from my little bed, and from my
    boredom,
from my mirrors, from my moon, from the closet
    of my life…from my shyness?

From "Homing Pigeons" by Mahmoud Darwish

Is a Jew a Palestinian? Is a Palestinian a Jew?
Where does one begin to answer such a question?
I will say this: we are cut from the same rock,
breathe the scent of the same lemons & olives,
anchor our troubles with the same stones,
carefully placed. We are *challah* & *hummus*, eaten
together to make a meal.

Anndee Hochman

ISS

The secret kiss grew larger and larger.

Liyana Abboud had just tasted her first kiss when her parents announced they were leaving the country. They were having a "family meeting" at the Country Time Diner in St. Louis, the place Liyana and her brother Rafik felt embarrassed in because their father usually returned his dinner for not being hot enough.

Of course no one knew about the kiss, which Liyana was carrying in a secret pouch right under her skin.

Dr. Kamal Abboud, whom they called Poppy, jumped right in. "What do you think about moving to Jerusalem and starting new lives?" His face cracked into its most contagious smile. He was handsome and lean, with rumpled black hair and dark eyes. Liyana's best friend, Claire, always said he looked more like a movie star than any of the other dads.

Liyana's mother, Susan, filled in the gaps, as usual. She had long brown hair, which she usually wore pulled back in a straight ponytail, hazel eyes, and a calm way of talking. "Our family has reached a crossroads. You"—she opened her hand toward Liyana—"are going into high school next year. You"—she pointed at Rafik—"are going into middle school. Once you get into your new schools, you will feel less like moving across the ocean. This is the best time we can think of to make the big change."

The kiss started burning a hole up through Liyana's smooth left cheek where it had begun. The blaze spread over to her lips where the kiss had ended. She could imagine her lips igniting over the menu.

"Wow!" Rafik said. He combed both his hands backward through his curly black hair, the way he always did when he was excited.

"Liyana, what are you looking at?" Poppy asked.

She hadn't smiled back yet. Her eyes were fixed on the floral wreath hanging over the cash register and her mouth tried to shape the words, "Maybe it's a bad idea," but nothing came out. She felt the same way she did after the car accident on an icy road last winter, when she'd noticed the Magic Marker stain on the seat instead of the blood coming out of her elbow. Stunned into observation.

Leave the country?

Of course it was a rumor Liyana had been hearing all her life. Someday her family would leave the United States, the country her mother and she and her brother had been born in, and move overseas to the mixed-up country her father had been born in. It was only fair. He wanted to show it to them. He wanted them to know both sides of their history and become the fully rounded human beings they were destined to be.

"You know," Poppy said, "I never planned to be an immigrant forever. I never thought I'd become a citizen. I planned to return home after medical school. I didn't know"—and here Rafik picked up the familiar refrain with him, like the chorus to "America the Beautiful"—*"I'd fall in love and stay for so many years."* Rafik covered his heart with his hand and closed his eyes. Poppy laughed.

Poppy wanted Liyana and Rafik to know Sitti, their grandmother. He would transfer to Al-Makassad Hospital in Jerusalem—he'd been in touch with them by mail and fax. Liyana and Rafik would have doubled lives. When Liyana was younger, she used to think this sounded like fun. That was long before last night's kiss.

———

The biggest surprise about the kiss was it didn't come from Phillip, the person on Liyana's right at the movie theater, who *might* have kissed her because they'd been good friends for years and she had a crush on him, but from Jackson, on her left.

Jackson was in her social studies class. Liyana liked the way he smelled—like Poppy's old bottle of English Leather. They'd traded notes about Mali and Ethiopia, and she complimented him on his enormous vocabulary. Sometimes they stood together in the lunch line, discussing the dazzling enchiladas, and they ate together, but not every day.

Jackson had leaned over to ask what the actress in the movie had just said and the next thing Liyana knew, his lips were nuzzling her cheek. They moved to her mouth and held there for a moment, pressing lightly.

Liyana had no idea what happened at the end of the movie. It was a swirling blue blur, like an underwater scene. Afterward, her friends crowded toward the exit doors, laughing. Jackson tripped over someone's empty popcorn tub on the floor. Liyana liked that he picked it up and threw it away. It said something about him. But they didn't talk much at Claire's pizza party, and all they said when Poppy picked Liyana up later was, "See you at school," as if nothing had happened.

Still, there was something different between them now. A little glimmer. His lips were so warm. Liyana had never imagined lips being warm.

———

And now she was leaving the country. The waitress refilled Poppy's tea.

"What will we do with our things?" mumbled Liyana. The piano; the blue bicycles; the boxes of tangle-haired dolls Liyana hadn't played with in years, though she refused to give them away; the mountains of books; the blackboard on an easel where she and Rafik left each other notes. It stood in the hallway between their rooms.

Did you take my red marker? Big trouble, buddy!
Red marker seized by Klingon intruders!

Who would they be if they had to start all over again? Liyana started thinking of the word "immigrant" in a different way at that moment and her skin prickled. Now *she* would be the immigrant.

Poppy curled his finger at the waitress. "Honey," he said to her. "My potato is positively icy inside."

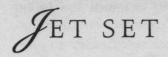

JET SET

*Some days were long sentences
flowing into one another.*

They flew to New York in steamy June, left their
seventeen suitcases and Liyana's violin stored at
the airport, and spent one day lugging stuffed
backpacks around to the Empire State Building
and riding up to the inside of the Statue of
Liberty's head. Poppy was retracing his steps. He
wanted them to see exactly what he had seen
when he first came to the United States.

"When Miss Liberty appeared through the fog
holding up her hand in the harbor, I felt she was
an old girlfriend welcoming me. I'd seen so many
pictures of her."

"It's not just a hand, Poppy, it's a *torch*," Rafik
said. His mother flashed him a quieting look. She
wanted Poppy to keep telling stories.

Poppy recalled, "When I saw a sign for hot
dogs, I thought they were made of dog meat. It
scared me. I thought the big shiny trash cans were
mailboxes."

Nineteen years after his first arrival, they ate

giant pretzels from a cart on the street. The big grains of salt on the pretzel skin tasted delicious. They bumped into disoriented families on summer vacations. They ate double scoops of Rocky Road ice cream.

"After this, you'll call ice cream *booza*," Poppy said. "And it won't have marshmallows, either. I don't think they've crossed the ocean yet."

"They'd get wet," said Rafik. Liyana rolled her eyes.

Liyana felt exhilarated by the skyscrapers. Their glittering lines lifted her out of her worry. She wished she could ride every sleek elevator up and down, punching buttons, seeing who got on and off. Some days you remembered the world was full of wonderful people you hadn't met yet. She bought seven postcards with different pictures—the Brooklyn Bridge, Washington Square, the fish market—imagining which one she might send to Jackson.

By the time they returned to the airport at sundown for their night flight overseas, a storm was swirling somewhere over the dark Atlantic. They heard rumors about it from passengers at the gate. Ominous booms of distant thunder made Liyana feel edgy inside. *Yippity loosebugs,* she thought. Their flight was running two hours late. Liyana kept her eyes on the other people waiting to fly. She wanted to see if they looked nervous.

But they only looked sleepy. A yawning lady with a flowered scarf tied under her chin lugged a food basket jammed with Jell-O boxes, paper napkins, and coffee filters. Didn't they have those things in the Middle East? Another lady rolled up her husband's raincoat and made her little children lie down on the floor with their heads on it. No one looked nervous at all.

When Rafik unzipped his backpack and pulled out a giant sack of Cornnuts, Liyana went to sit at the other side of the gate. She couldn't stand to sit next to somebody crunching. She scribbled in her notebook. *One Indian lady in a purple sari crying. The size of good-bye.*

CLOVER CHAIN

Some days I am brave,
but other days I almost disappear.

Before the Abboud family left St. Louis, there were
many times Liyana thought she would rather be
anyone else on their block, someone who planned to
stick around in the neighborhood doing dull things
like going to Mannino's grocery store and staring at
watermelons and jars of peanut butter stacked up.
She would rather *not* have to change her life.

She knew the bush with red berries that were
probably poison. She knew which bus number to
take downtown. Often the Abboud family drove
around on slow Sunday evenings with their car
windows wide open to "smell the air." That's what
Poppy said people did in Jerusalem.

St. Louis air smelled of tar and doughnuts, old
boards washed up out of the muddy river, red
bricks, and licorice. Leafy greens of bushes and
trees ran together outside their car. How could
Liyana give all this up? She knew what grass
smelled like, a rich brew of dirt and green roots,
right after rain.

And her fingers knew exactly the best way to twist skinny green clover stems together to make a long chain to stretch across the street to stop cars. She would stand on one side and Rafik would stand on the other, holding his end for as long as he could pay attention.

Of course the cars could have driven right through the chain if they tried. Most drivers would laugh and motion for Liyana and Rafik to pull the chain back. But one day right after they started telling people they were moving overseas, a man in a red pickup truck slammed on his brakes, shook his fist from the window, and shouted that he'd tell the police and make them pay a fine.

"We are children!" Liyana called out. He glared at her then. They dropped the chain and he drove away.

"Could he really do that?" Rafik asked.

"Let's go in," Liyana said. "I don't want to play."

LIP

Being little was a skin that fit.

It had seemed to Liyana that Poppy was walking differently during the weeks before they left. His stride had a new lift in it. He made lots of overseas phone calls. Mrs. Abboud would watch him and raise ten fingers like a coach or a referee when she thought he should get off.

But he also kept falling into silent spells. At the dinner table he forgot to remove the blue denim baseball cap he wore for yard work. He wasn't combing his hair as carefully as usual. When he read a newspaper story about demonstrations in Jerusalem, he rolled the newspaper into a tube and slapped it against his arm.

"What's up?" Liyana asked him as he poured gasoline into the lawn mower for the last time. He jumped. "Are you worried we're making a mistake?"

"No," he said. "I was just thinking about…how I like doing this."

She caught him staring at odd things—the hinge on the pantry cabinet, the medicine chest in the bathroom. When she asked what he was doing, he said, "Remembering."

Liyana, too, had been trying to memorize at least one small detail about each house on their street. The blue cottage with the crooked chimney, the green two-story only half painted. Did the painters break their arms? Did they lose their enthusiasm for that color? The brick house with the pink vine wrapped around its forehead in the summers. Liyana might never see the cherry trees or tulip beds or gray pebbles or cracked sidewalks again.

When she was younger, before she went to middle school and her arms seemed to grow longer in the night, she knew the easy latitude and longitude of her world. Now she was moving away to a land she knew little of, except the skillet of olive oil with crumbles of garlic and pine nuts browning on the stove. Liyana's mother stood over the skillet with the spatula poised, like a scientist. Poppy would pass through the house lifting his nose to the air, saying, "There it is, there's my country."

Well, where was hers? Was she on the verge of finding out? Sometimes Liyana felt she had passed her own country already and it was an age, not a place.

She wrote it down in her notebook.

An age, not a place.

What did it mean, exactly?

Liyana loved thinking of first lines for stories or poems or movies.

Since fourth grade, she'd kept a running list of them and liked to reread it to see if she could get the stories to go further in her head.

The secret kiss grew larger and larger.

No one had dialed her number for a dozen years.

If she had known her cousin's secret, would she have teased her at dinner?

Sometimes she took her lists of lines to Mrs. Lindenwood, her old fourth-grade teacher who loved creative writing, and Mrs. Lindenwood would put stars by the ones she liked best. Or Liyana would read them to Poppy in the yard after they'd washed the dinner dishes, as he sat drinking a cup of Arabic coffee in his favorite green metal chair with the scalloped back. On one of their last evenings in St. Louis, Poppy said, "Tell *me* her cousin's secret!"

Liyana hadn't read him the one about the kiss.

"Sometimes you remind me of Sitti, my mother," he told her.

"Why?" Liyana had a little picture of Sitti in her wallet, standing in a long dress in the archway entrance to her house.

"Making something out of nothing. It's her

favorite thing to do. She gets a whole story out of—a button. Or a rock."

Liyana was quiet. She flicked at a mosquito, thinking how people considered other people. Did other people think *she* was strange? Sitti was eighty and Poppy said her mother had lived to be ninety-nine. What if it ran in the family?

Liyana and Poppy sat silently in the backyard while their gray cat, Sami, leaped down from the top of the wooden fence to bury his nose in the grass. Sami was going to live at their aunt's house, but Rafik and Liyana worried she might forget to feed him. They had discussed giving him tranquilizers and stowing him away in a backpack.

Liyana asked Poppy, "Do you remember that Emily Dickinson poem I liked a lot in second grade that starts, 'I'm nobody, who are you?'"

"Sort of. But I never thought you were nobody."

"I'm even more nobody now than I was then."

"Oh *habibti,* don't say that! You're everything you need to be!"

"Poppy, remember when you told us your twentieth birthday was the most important landmark day of your life? I do *not* think it will be a very good day in mine."

"That's okay. You're only fourteen. You have a lot of time. And I only meant it was the landmark day of my life till *then*. I've had *lots* of better landmarks since. Like the days you and Rafik were born! And every day after! Twenty was just a little—blip—now that I look back on it."

Liyana wrote down what he said. *"A little blip—now that I look back on it."* She closed her notebook as Sami ran toward them with a lizard in his mouth.

ESTATE SALE

Their family was half and half,
like a carton of rich milk.

Liyana and Rafik had tucked three apology notes into mailboxes in their neighborhood. Sorry to Mrs. Moore for borrowing her daisies more than once. Sorry to Lucy Hummer for calling her a witch after Rafik's ball skipped into her yard and she kept it a week before pitching it back. Sorry to Frank for leaving a sign on the windshield of his antique station wagon without wheels that said HUNK OF JUNK.

Their mother was having problems with her own mother, Peachy Helen, Liyana and Rafik's other grandmother, who lived by Forest Park in a high-rise apartment. Peachy wore flowery dresses and high spots of blush on her cheeks and she couldn't *stand* it that they were leaving. She was addicted to their after-school phone calls. She was used to dropping in at a moment's notice. She stayed with Liyana and Rafik when their parents went out of town. She and Liyana often ate lunch together on Saturdays at fancy ladies' tearooms.

They chose custard pies off the gleaming dessert cart.

After she heard they were moving, Peachy Helen kept crying. She even hung up on Liyana so she wouldn't hear her cry. This cast a dim glow on Liyana's mother, who suddenly had trouble finishing sentences and meals. She would leap up from the table, thinking of more things she needed to do.

———

Liyana and Rafik lettered poster-board signs for the Estate Sale while their mother gathered stacks of yellowed newspapers from the corners, throwing them into recycling bins. "I would hardly call this an estate," she said dubiously. But the woman at the newspaper who copied down their ad had been adamant—a "Garage Sale" meant you carried things outside and an "Estate Sale" meant you sold the whole household from the inside out.

Harpsichord music blared from Liyana's cassette player. Liyana said, "Estate Sale sounds disgraceful to me, as if we're planning to display stained baby clothes and sticky ketchup bottles! I hate it!"

She worried, What if Jackson came? What if he saw the dumbo Pretty Princess game with half its jewels missing in the bargain bin? What if her girlfriends pawed through her threadbare socks,

Nancy Drew mysteries, and frayed hair ribbons, casting them aside and choosing none?

Her mother arranged sale items on long folding tables they'd rented and urged Liyana and Rafik to get their suitcases organized, all at once. Liyana packed a pink diary with a key, the Scrabble game, and a troll with rhinestone eyes, collecting other childhood treasures—the Mexican china tea set, the stuffed monkeys—to leave boxed up in Peachy Helen's already-stuffed closets and in a friend's barn. She arranged a small box of odd treasures—stones, butterfly wings, a carved wooden toad—to give to Claire.

Liyana sorted through perfect spelling tests and crackly finger paintings from a box under her bed. She folded the red velvet embroidered dress that her faraway relatives had stitched for her long ago. It had arrived in the mail wrapped in heavy paper, with twine knotted around it. Now she was going to meet the fingers that knotted the thread. She polished her violin, placing it tenderly back in its case with the white cloth over its neck. She considered whether to take an extra cake of rosin along with new strings. There was so much to think about when you moved.

Rafik tried to throw his old report cards away, but their mother caught him. Who even *cared* about the minuses on his old conduct grades by now? If the cards went into the barn boxes, mice might chew them up. The *E*'s and *S*'s could turn into dust.

Rafik agonized at length over his beloved Matchbox car collection. He lined fire trucks and emergency vehicles on one side of his bed and vans and trucks with movable doors on the other side. Poppy had said he could take ten or twenty. Rafik felt nauseated trying to decide which ones he'd have to abandon. Liyana, passing his room with another cardboard box in her arms, found him poking race cars into his socks.

"So let me pick for you," she offered. He shook his head, knowing she had a strange preference for milk trucks and tractors. Liyana left him alone and pitched the box onto her bed.

———

Poppy poked his head through Liyana's doorway. "You won't need those shorts," he said. "No one wears shorts over there."

"That's not true! I've seen pictures of Jerusalem and some people are definitely wearing shorts."

"They're tourists. Maybe they're pilgrims. We're going to be spending time in older places where shorts won't be *appropriate*. Believe me, Arab women don't wear shorts." He walked away.

Lately Poppy kept bringing up Arab women and it made Liyana mad. "I'm not a woman or a full Arab, either one!" She slammed her bedroom door, knowing what would happen next. Poppy would enter, stand with hands on his hips, and say, "Would you like to tell me something?"

Liyana muttered, "I'm just a half-half, woman-girl, Arab-American, a mixed breed like those wild characters that ride up on ponies in the cowboy movies Rafik likes to watch. The half-breeds are always villains or rescuers, never anybody normal in between."

She rolled six socks into balls and found some old birthday cards tucked beneath them. Then she had to read the cards.

Poppy knocked on her door.

Liyana opened it and threw her arms around him. "I'm sorry, dear Poppy. What if I don't take my very short shorts? What if I only take the baggy checkered old-man shorts that come down to my knees?"

He shrugged, hugging her back. "Maybe you can wear them when we visit the Dead Sea." That was the sea so full of salt, you could sit upright in it as if it were a chair.

Liyana gave her short shorts to Sandee Lane, her friend down the block who kept saying how great it was that they were going to live in

"Jesus's hometown." Liyana didn't think of it that way. She thought of it as her *dad's* hometown.

———

"Where did all these people *come from?*" Rafik whispered during the Estate Sale.

He and Liyana sat behind a bush next to their house in the thinnest, softest grass watching customers travel up the sidewalk. They must have driven in from other neighborhoods. Thankfully, no one looked familiar.

One woman carried out their dented metal mixing bowl. A man pulled Poppy's lovely green wheelbarrow behind him. Liyana covered her eyes. "Oh! I'll miss that wheelbarrow."

She thought of all the things she *couldn't* pack, imagining the slim green locker she would have had at high school next year if she weren't moving to the other side of the ocean. She thought of Lonnie and Kelly and Barbara, her friends, just starting to streak their lips with pale lipstick for special events. She and Claire didn't, because they thought it was dumb. "Lucky you!" Claire had said. "You'll miss the tryouts for youth symphony next season."

"Lucky you!" Lonnie had said. "There are really cute guys in Jerusalem. I've seen them on CNN."

"Lucky nothing." Liyana had said private

good-byes to the third step outside the school cafeteria where she ate when the weather was nice and the chute at the library where she'd poured her books since she was five and the fragrant pine needles on the trees between their house and the Ferraris'. Liyana and her friends used to make forts on the ground inside those branches.

Liyana and Rafik had never yet found out what animal lived in the hole by the back sidewalk. It wasn't a mole—moles made big mounds in the middle of the yard. How could they leave when it still hadn't come out?

Rafik poked her, whispering, "I am NOT BELIEVING this! Look at that! Someone just bought my Dracula Halloween costume, the ugliest costume on earth! I was *sure* it wouldn't sell!"

<hr>

That evening their house looked stripped. A few large pieces of furniture people would pick up the next day wore red tags with names and phone numbers on them. The piano was going to live with MERTON at 555–3232.

Their mother played Mozart the night before the piano left. Liyana noticed she wasn't keeping her ponytail pulled back neatly in its silver clip as she usually did. Loose strands of hair cluttered the sides of her elegant face.

"Amazing," she called out to Liyana in her bare room, "that Mozart could write this when he was six and I have trouble playing it when I'm forty."

Liyana could play one line better than her mother could. She got up from bed to show her and was startled to see tears gleaming on Mom's cheeks. She placed her hands alongside on the keyboard.

"Your hands are more like your father's," her mother always said.

Liyana's hands and feet peeled in the springtime like Poppy's did, an inherited genetic trait. She didn't sweat, either.

"Why couldn't you have kept the piano?" Liyana said. "You could have stored it somewhere. Couldn't Peachy Helen have fit it into her apartment?"

There were only a few things Liyana's mother was attached to.

"Clean slate," Mom said, as if they were talking in code, and Liyana said, "Huh?"

"We are starting over." Her mother's voice was so thin and wavery, it scared her.

She was usually so upbeat about things. Liyana and Rafik teased her about being the general of the Optimist's Army. *Positive thoughts, ho! Forward march!* Liyana thought her words turned up at the ends, like elf shoes. "Look for the Silver Lining" was her mother's favorite song. She made Liyana and Rafik memorize it. Their mother wouldn't even let them say things like "bad weather." She wouldn't look at a newspaper till afternoon because she didn't want bad news setting the tone for the day. Peachy Helen, on the other hand, crouched over the newspaper on her kitchen table, moaning over kidnappings, hijackings, and hurricanes as if each one were personal. "I can't stop thinking about Sarah's mother," Peachy said once.

"Who's Sarah?"

"The girl who drowned in Colorado."

This was some poor person Peachy and the Abbouds had never *met*.

Liyana's mother placed her American hand over Liyana's half-half one on the keyboard. "Go to bed. You're going to need all the sleep you can get."

On their last night in St. Louis, the neighborhood gave the Abboud family a going-away party in their front yard. The FOR SALE sign on the house had a red SOLD slapped across it. Liyana licked custard from a cream puff and stared at their familiar, rumpled neighbors in their summer clothes. They'd be around all summer and Liyana's family would not. She eavesdropped on everybody—eavesdropping was her specialty. Talk about camp and favorite teachers and the opening of the neighborhood swimming pool made her feel wistful.

She tried to remember the exact sensation of Jackson's kiss, but it was dissolving in her mind. She wished she had thought to invite him to this. But he might not have come, and that would have been worse. Claire dropped a small velvet ring box into Liyana's hand at the last minute and ran home crying. A tightly folded note tucked under a silver friendship ring said, "I will never *ever* forget you."

CIVILIZED

I vote for the cat sleeping in the sun.

When the weary passengers finally boarded the giant jet at Kennedy Airport and it lifted off the runway, her mother clutched Liyana's wrist hard. "Oh my," she whispered. She closed her eyes.

Liyana pressed her face to the window and looked down. Every little light of New York City was a period at the end of a sentence. A dusty silver sheen in the sky capped the city as it shrank behind them. The airplane dipped and shivered. Liyana had only flown short flights to Kansas City and Chicago before. She had never flown across an ocean.

After they reached their transatlantic altitude, Poppy took pillows and fuzzy blue blankets down from the overhead bins. Flight attendants moved up the aisles handing out bedtime cups of water. Rafik already had his head tipped off to one side, eyes shuttered, and mouth slightly open. Liyana couldn't believe it. He could sleep anywhere, even with his life changing in the middle of a stormy sky. Liyana couldn't imagine sleeping now. She pressed the button over her seat so a sharp circle of light fell onto her lap. She wrote in her notebook, *"Do overnight pilots drink coffee? Do they take turns napping? A new chapter begins in the dark."*

—⁓—

Even her teachers back home had been nicer to her when they knew she was leaving. "Why don't you tell us about where you're going?" Mr. Hathaway, her history teacher, had said the last week of school. He had never liked Liyana since the day she let Claire, who sat behind her, French-braid her hair in class. "Of course we all *know* about Jerusalem—it's such a big part of religious history and constantly in the news—but why do you think people have had so much trouble acting *civilized* over there?"

Civilized was his favorite word. Once when Mr. Hathaway said people were and animals weren't, Liyana raised her hand.

"Just—look at the front page of any newspaper," she said nervously. It was harder to speak with a whole class staring at you. "Look at the words—for what people do: *attack, assault, molest, devastate, infiltrate.*"

He raised one eyebrow.

Liyana continued, "And that's just one page!"

When he invited her to write an essay about

Jerusalem for extra credit and read it to the class, she gulped. "It's a pretty big story." Crazy words came into her mind. *Yakkity boondocks. Flippery fidgets.*

"Interview your father...make some informal notes," Mr. Hathaway said. "Just use your own information—no encyclopedias for this! It may be your last chance for extra credit, you know."

JERUSALEM: A BIT OF THE STORY

When my father was growing up inside the Old City of Jerusalem—that's the ancient part of town inside the stone wall—he and the kids on his street liked to trade desserts after dinner.

My father would take his square of Arabic hareesa, a delicious cream-of-wheat cake with an almond balanced in the center, outside on a plate. His Jewish friend Avi from next door brought slices of date rolls. And a Greek girl named Anna would bring a plate of honey puffs or butter cookies. Everybody liked everyone else's dessert better than their own. So they'd trade back and forth. Sometimes they traded two ways at once.

Everybody was mixed together. My father says nobody talked or thought much about being Arabs or Jews or anything, they just ate, slept, studied, got in trouble at school, wore shoes with holes in the bottoms, hiked to Bethlehem on the weekends, and "heard the donkeys' feet grow fewer in the stone streets as the world filled up with cars." That's a direct quote.

But then, my father says, "the pot on the stove boiled over." That's a direct quote, too. After the British weren't in control anymore, the Jews wanted control and the Arabs wanted control. Everybody said Jerusalem and Palestine was theirs. Too many other countries, especially the United States, got involved with money, guns, and bossing around. Life became terrible for the regular people. A Jewish politician named Golda Meir said the Palestinian people never existed even though there were hundreds of thousands of them living all around her.

My father used to wish the politicians making big decisions would trade desserts. It might have helped. He would stand on his flat roof staring off to the horizon, thinking things must be better somewhere else. Even when he was younger, he asked himself, "Isn't it dumb to want only to be next to people who are just like you?"

Rifles blasted. Stone houses were blown up. They were old houses, too, the kind you think should stand forever. My father's best Arab friend of his whole childhood was killed next to him on a bench when they were both just sitting there. He won't talk about it. My mother told me. My father remembers church bells ringing before that moment. Because of this, church bells have always made him nervous.

Everyone in my father's family prayed for the

troubles to be solved. Probably the Jewish and Greek families were doing exactly the same thing. They held candlelight vigils in the streets. They carried large pictures of loved ones who had died. Everybody prayed that Jerusalem would have peace.

One night, when gunfire exploded near their house, Sitti, my grandmother, cried out to my father and his brothers, "Help! What should we do?"

My father said, "I don't know about you, but I'm covering my head."

And he did.

He says he just wasn't interested in fighting. He was applying for scholarships so he could get out of that mess. Sometimes he still feels guilty, like he ran away when there was trouble, but other times he's glad he left when he did. He always hoped to go back someday.

During those bad troubles, my father's family traveled north to a small village to stay with relatives. Sitti was too scared to stay home. Weeks later, they returned to Jerusalem to find their house "occupied"—filled with other people—Jewish soldiers with guns. Later the "Occupied Territories" indicated Palestinian lands that were seized by Israelis, so "occupied" became a nasty word.

My father's family went back to the village and moved into a big old house there, but they lost all the things inside their Jerusalem house. They lost their furniture and their dishes and their blankets and never got anything back. The Jewish soldiers with guns wouldn't let them. The bank wouldn't give them their money either. So it was really hard.

I don't understand how these things happen, personally. I'm just telling you what my father told me.

Other Palestinians ended up crowded together in refugee camps, which still exist today. They lived in little shacks, thinking they would be there only a short time. Unfortunately that wasn't true.

My father got his scholarship to study medicine in the United States and his family was not happy. They didn't want him to leave. He promised he would come back someday. It was hard for him to watch the evening news all these years. Sometimes the Middle East segments show people he knows. In medical school, he specialized in the care of old people because young people were too mixed up. Maybe he should have become a vet.

Then he met my mother, an American, which is why he stayed over here so long. Stories of the American Indians made my father very sad. He knew how they felt.

Only recently he grew hopeful about Jerusalem and his country again. Things started changing for the better. Palestinians had public voices again. Of course they never stopped having private voices. That's something you can't take away from people. My father says, wouldn't you think the Jews, because of the tragedies they went through in Europe themselves, would have remembered this? Some did. But they weren't always the powerful ones.

The Arabs and Jews shook hands again, at the White House and in lots of other places, too. Many of them had never stopped doing it, secretly. Of course some people believed in the peace process more than others. Can you imagine why anyone would not? I can't.

That's when my father began planning for us to move back. He wants us to know our relatives. He wants to be in his old country as it turns into a better country. If it doesn't work out, we can always return to the United States.

I think of it as an adventure. I will miss all of you, especially Mr. Hathaway's pop quizzes and Clayton's fascinating monologues about mummies. If I become one, I hope you all will be fortunate enough to dig me up.

P.S. to Mr. Hathaway—that last part was just a joke.

Liyana Abboud

$\mathcal{P}$ALS

*Are dreams thinner at
thirty-three thousand feet?*

When their plane landed at Tel Aviv, Poppy was talking so fast, Liyana couldn't pay close attention to details. Normally she liked to notice trees first—their leaves and shapes—when she arrived in a new place. Then she'd focus on plants, signs, and, gradually, people. Liyana believed in working up to people. But Poppy leaned across the aisle jabbering so fast, she could barely notice the color of the sky.

"When we go through the checkpoint for passports, let me do the talking, okay? We don't let them stamp our passports here. They stamp a little piece of paper instead. And don't leave anything on the plane. Look around! Did you check under the seats? We'll go to the hotel first and rest awhile, then we'll call the village. My family will come in to see us. They won't expect us to travel all the way out to visit them today. Make sure you have everything. Did you get those pistachios? What about that book Rafik was reading?"

"Poppy's nervous," her mother whispered to

Liyana. "He hasn't been here in five years."

He was making Liyana nervous, too. *Jitterbug bazooka.* He didn't like it when she said foolish words lined up, like *mousetrap taffy-puller.* That's what she did inside her head when she got nervous. Poppy hadn't told his family their exact arrival time on purpose. "They don't need to come to the airport and make a big scene," he said.

Powder-puff peanut. She'd be good. She wouldn't talk at Customs. She wouldn't say, *Yes I'm carrying my worst American habits in the zipper pouch of my suitcase and I plan to let them loose in your streets. There's a kiss in there, too! I'll never tell.*

Right away, the Israeli agents singled Liyana's family out and made them stand off to the side in a troublemaker line with two men who looked like international zombies. Other travelers—sleek Spaniards, Irish nuns—zoomed right through. The women soldiers at the gate seemed meaner than the men. They all wore dull khaki uniforms. Big guns swung on straps across their backs.

Poppy had said this singling-out treatment often happened to Palestinians, even Palestinian-Americans, but one of Poppy's Palestinian friends had had a better arrival recently, when an Israeli customs agent actually said to him, "Welcome home." Poppy said it depended on what good or bad thing had just happened in the news.

Five years before, when Poppy had traveled here with his friend Mustafa, a Palestinian-American psychiatrist, the customs officer held them up so long at the gate, checking every corner of their suitcases and interrogating them so severely, that Mustafa leaned over, kissed the officer on the cheek, and said, "Let's just be friends, okay?" The Israeli man had been so stunned to be kissed that he waved them both through. And the two of them laughed all the way to Jerusalem.

Today the guard chose his words carefully. "Why are you planning to *stay* here?" Poppy had written "indefinitely" on the length of their visit when he filled out the papers on the plane. The papers were so boring. Liyana thought of more interesting questions they might ask. *What's the best word you ever made in Scrabble?*

She heard her father explain, in an unusually high-pitched tone, "I happen to be *from here,* and I am moving back. I have a job waiting for me at the hospital. I am introducing my family to my country and to their relatives. If you will notice, I have taken care of all the necessary paperwork at the embassy in the United States." He jingled some coins in his pocket. Liyana worried for him. He only jingled coins when he was upset.

The airport guards checked through their suitcases and backpacks extremely carefully. They lifted each item high in the air and stared at it. They wheeled the empty bags away on a cart to be x-rayed. They placed things back in a jumble. Liyana's flowered raggedy underpants fell to the floor and she scooped them up, embarrassed. The guards did not care for her violin. They looked inside its sound hole and shook it, hard. They jabbered fast in Hebrew.

Rafik tried to set his watch by a giant clock on the wall. He said, too loudly, "This airport seems ugly," and their mother shushed him. It was true. The walls were totally gray. There were no welcome posters, no murals, no candy stands. Three other stern-looking guards moved in closer to Liyana's family. Did they think they were going to start a riot or something? The guards looked ready to jump on them. Liyana felt a knot tightening in her stomach.

Maybe one reason their father wanted them to be quiet is they had trouble calling this country "Israel" to begin with. Why? Because Poppy had always, forever and ever, called it Palestine. Why wouldn't he? That's what he called it as a little boy. It was "Palestine" for the first years of his life and that's how most Arabs still referred to it to this day. Maybe he was afraid his family would slip.

In the airplane, somewhere over the Mediterranean, Liyana had whispered to Rafik, "Too bad the country namers couldn't have made some awful combo word from the beginning, like *Is-Pal* or *Pal-Is,* to make everybody happy."

Rafik said, "Huh?"

"But hardly anybody there has been pals yet."

"Are you going crazy?"

"And Pal-Is sounds like palace—but they don't even have a king. Do you think they would have been better off with kings?"

Later when the guard at the customs gate pointed at Rafik and asked Liyana weirdly, "Is this your brother?" as if he might be a stranger she'd just picked up in the air, she was moved to say, "He *is* my *pal*," and they both started giggling, which made Poppy glare at them worriedly.

The guard sighed. He couldn't find any reason to detain them further. He shoved the passports back at Poppy. "You may go on."

WELCOME

*She opened her mouth
and a siren came out.*

At the hotel in Jerusalem, Liyana sat on the lumpy couch staring at her blue passport. *Given name, nationality, date of birth...*she turned herself upside down. She had braided her dark brown hair the day she got the picture taken. Now she wished she hadn't. One braid was fatter than the other. She thought her large eyes looked too hopeful, like the eyes of a dog.

Rafik bounded into the room with two glasses of freshly squeezed lemonade in his hands. His long, checkered shirttail was hanging out of his pants. "You should see it down there!" he babbled excitedly. "There's a real live sheep tied up right outside the back door of this hotel! I touched its head and it went *baaa-aaa!* Then I saw mysterious carving in a stone on the floor by the restaurant! It looks like a code! Was this place here when Jesus was?"

"Goofball!" Liyana said. They downed their lemonades in three great gulps each.

Poppy kept talking a mile a minute as they

waited for Sitti and the family to appear. He unpacked his travel kit and sprayed on fresh cologne. He combed his thick hair back from his forehead and stared into a mirror, probably for the first time in weeks. Then he turned to them and placed his hands together.

"Remember, Sitti comes from a different world. She's very—earthy. She doesn't wear anything but old-fashioned long clothes and she never did. She may seem strange to you. You won't understand her. I'll translate whatever you need, since she knows absolutely nothing in English—"

Liyana interrupted—"As little as we know in Arabic?"—and her mother hushed her.

Poppy continued without blinking, "They'll want us to come out to the village tonight to eat, but look, it's a twenty-eight-mile drive one way and it's four P.M. already. I'll say you're tired from the long flight. All right? If we go to the village, a hundred people will be pouring into the house to see us. It's too much for tonight. Is everyone okay?"

Liyana said, "We used to be okay, till you started making us so nervous!" She whispered to Rafik, "Does he think they won't like us? Does he think we won't like them?"

Rafik lay on the bed, sighing happily. He said, "Have you felt these pillows? They're the deepest pillows in the world!"

Liyana lay down on the next bed. Her head sank into the soft feathers and she said, "You're right." Then she got up again and changed from her blue corduroy pants to her pleated black skirt. She was thinking how amazing it was that people could get on an airplane and step off again in a different universe.

After Poppy had peeked out the window twenty times at taxis veering by with honking horns and squealing tires and their mother had combed and recombed her hair, applying a new dash of perky red lipstick, everyone finally arrived. Their babbling echoes filled the lobby before they got on the elevator. Poppy stepped outside the door to greet them.

Then a huge crowd of relatives burst into the room, bustling, hugging, pinching cheeks, and jabbering loudly. They were smoky smelling, not like cigarette smoke but the deeper smoke of a campfire that goes into clothes and stays there after the fire's out.

Indeed, they were not like any relatives Liyana had ever met before. In the United States their extended family (except for Peachy Helen, who always acted cozy) held back from them politely as if they might have a cold. Uncle Leo had never hugged Liyana yet. He shook her hand like an insurance man. Aunt Margaret spoke formally to children, about general subjects. *Are you enjoying the summer? Do you have nice friends?*

But this bustling group of aunts and uncles swirled in circles as Sitti, their grandmother, threw her strong arms around each one of them in succession, squeezing so tightly that Liyana lost her breath. "She's blessing you," Poppy whispered.

Liyana had an impulse to stand very close to Poppy, for protection, and also for translation, so he could keep her posted on what was being said. Tears poured down Sitti's rugged cheeks. Suddenly she threw her head back, rolled her tongue high up in her mouth, and began trilling wildly. Liyana had never heard anything like it. Aunt Saba and Aunt Amal began clapping a rhythmic beat. Mom looked startled. Rafik raised his eyebrows.

Poppy shook his head, waving both hands in Sitti's face to quiet her down. "That's her traditional cry," he explained. "She uses it as an announcement at weddings and—funerals."

"Which one is *this*?" Liyana asked.

Poppy spoke rapidly to Sitti in Arabic, but she didn't stop right away. She trilled and trilled and trilled. She shimmied her arms in the air like a Pentecostal preacher. The backs of her hands were tattooed with the dark blue shapes of flying birds.

Liyana said, "Poppy! You never told us she had tattoos!"

Poppy said, "I didn't want you to get any ideas."

"I'm considering an eagle, myself," Rafik said.

Sitti pulled Poppy's face close to hers again and again to kiss him on both cheeks. Liyana liked that. Two kisses seemed better than one.

Liyana was being kissed by so many people whose exact identity was unknown to her, though Poppy tried to clarify names of aunts, cousins, and wives of cousins, to help his family out. Even he had trouble. He gave two different names for the same woman and everyone laughed. Liyana kept nodding and trying to kiss people back, even when she missed their cheeks. She kissed Aunt Lena on the scarf and felt silly. Still, after all that flying, the enthusiastic welcome was nice. At least Liyana knew they had landed in the proper hemisphere.

The women's long dresses were made of thick fabrics, purple, gold, and navy blue, and stitched brightly with fabulous, complicated embroidery. Aunt Lena had rich lines of multicolored rainbow thread wrapped around her wrists. All the women wore gold bangle bracelets. The older ones had long white scarves draped and knotted firmly over their hair. The younger ones had bare heads, which made Liyana feel relieved.

They wore plastic, slip-on shoes in pastel colors. The modern shoes seemed strange with their old-fashioned clothes. Aunt Saba touched Liyana's blue-and-yellow Swiss children's watch that had little people's heads on the ends of its hands. She put her face down to stare at it and laughed. The women even touched Liyana's earlobes. She wore no gold earrings, as they did. But Liyana didn't mind. She didn't feel like a "specimen." She liked their curiosity. The men wore dull gray or black suits, white shirts, and striped ties, more like men anywhere. Liyana wondered how men ever got such boring uniforms, anyway. Sometimes she looked at encyclopedia pages showing "native dress" styles from around the world. Elsewhere, in Zambia maybe, or Timbuktu, the men knew how to dress. In the older days, Arab men wore long, flowing robes and cloaks with golden edges, but suits had sneaked into their closets now. Poppy had told Liyana she would like the men's elegant clothing in Saudi Arabia and the United Arab Emirates better.

Two of the older uncles, Zaki and Daoud, wore black-and-white-checkered *kaffiyehs* on their heads, which made them look more interesting. Liyana liked their weather-beaten brown faces immediately. Rafik was tugging at her elbow. He whispered, "Does that mean his name is *Daoud Abboud?*"

Liyana said, "I think he's married to one of our aunts. He must have a different last name. But let's not find out what it is right now, okay? My head is spinning!"

Poppy translated what Aunt Amal said, about how scary it had been for them to pass the Israeli checkpoint when they entered Jerusalem. Her face looked alarmed. All four taxis filled with family members had been stopped. They'd been asked to show special permits they had secured two days ago. The Israeli soldier shouted at them and they got scared. He had a gun. He threw Uncle Daoud's pass on the ground because it was slightly bent and made him get out of the car to pick it up. When he was done looking at the passes, Sitti thought he said, "Go away," but he meant, "Go on."

Liyana noticed her mother's face turning worried as Poppy translated. Her mother fingered the edge of Sitti's sleeve. "What?" Liyana asked her. "What are you thinking of?"

"I thought things were supposed to be much better now."

"That's not what they're telling me," Poppy said. "They say the rules change every two days. And they almost never come into the city anymore."

Rafik said, "I think the same person just kissed me for the tenth time."

Poppy rubbed his hands together. "We should go downstairs to get some tea or coffee." Liyana knew he was trying to lighten the atmosphere, but a huge babble broke loose. "They aren't used to hotels," he explained.

In fact, today was the first time *in her life* Sitti had ever ridden in an elevator. Always before, in any building with more than one floor, she insisted on taking the stairs. Sitti said little boxes were for dead people. She didn't want to enter the elevator today, either, and they had to push her.

Liyana noticed the women of the family eyeing her mother closely. She was an inch taller than Poppy, and her skin two shades lighter. Liyana and Rafik had inherited Poppy's olive skin. *Did they think her mother was pretty?* They seemed to like her mother's long hair. They all had long hair, too, braided, or knotted in buns. Liyana guessed the ones with scarves had long, hidden hair. Everyone must have wondered about a woman who could have kept a man from living in his own country till now. They must have had mixed feelings.

Liyana's mother kept smiling widely at them, placing her hands on top of theirs like in that game for babies where the bottom hand keeps getting pulled out. Beyond the window, cars and trucks of Jerusalem swerved and honked, screeching their brakes and wailing up to the curb. Rafik, peeking out the window at her side, said, "Have you noticed how many old Mercedes Benzes there are here?" Her brain swirled with names, *Lena, Saba, Leila,* ending in *a,* like her own. Would she ever get them straight?

Suddenly, just as everyone headed out the door for a tea party, Rafik vomited on the floor.

Mrs. Abboud rushed toward the bathroom for tissues, which were so small and thin that she threw them up in the air when she returned. What about bath towels? Awful. "Liyana," she hissed. "Move! Help!" Poppy broke the momentary frozen spell by waving his hands to urge everyone out into the hall. Whenever he saw anyone vomit, he felt nauseated himself.

Rafik stumbled toward the bathroom. Liyana followed, saying, "Are you sick?"

He said, "No, dope-dope, that's how we say hello in my language. What do you think?"

Their mother buzzed the hotel desk to ask for a mop, but the clerk brought a broom instead. Then he ran for wet rags. Liyana sat with Rafik on the edge of the bathtub, considering aloud details of the last three meals they had eaten, to his horror. "Could it have been the cucumber on the plane? The little scrap of tomato in your sandwich?"

"Could you please please please keep your mouth shut?"

When he didn't throw up again, but began smiling weakly and making jokes, their mother produced antinausea tablets from her medicine bag, told Rafik please to rest and take it easy, asked Liyana to stay with him, and went downstairs to join the family.

Liyana lay on the other twin bed, idly reciting, "One potato, two potato, three potato, four..."

Rafik said, "Did anyone ever tell you you're mean?"

FIRST THINGS LAST

*Her own first things
kept lasting longest in her brain.*

Rafik fell asleep on top of his white bedspread immediately, so Liyana shut her eyes on her bed, too, and
plummeted into a frozen scene. She dreamed she was
standing at the top of the steepest hill in Forest Park,
St. Louis, in front of the art museum, on a fresh
morning of new snow. No one else was out yet.

She held her wooden sled by its rope, trying to
decide whether to jump onto it and swoop down
the slope, but it was hard to do when your sled's
runners would be the first to mark the surface.
Better to watch someone else doing it first—otherwise you weren't sure how fast you would go.

The horse statue was iced like a cookie. Bare
trees poked their bony arms into the sky. At the
bottom of the hill, the frozen lake glistened in the
light. Liyana wore a nubby brown coat that hadn't
fit her in years. She'd kept it in the back of her closet
till recently and felt sad, after the estate sale, that it
was gone forever. She wore her turquoise mittens

with a long cord connecting them, running up her sleeves and across her back to keep them together.

How old was she in this dream, three? She was biting her lip hard, the way she used to do to make a decision.

Although she'd thought she was alone in the snow, someone pushed her abruptly from behind and she plopped onto the sled, shrieking, flailing down the slope on her stomach. Who did that, Rafik? But Rafik would still have been a baby then. The sled was soaring. It became a rocket ship, a dizzy runaway. She couldn't steer for a minute. The rope flew out behind her. What if she crashed into the lake? What if the ice broke? She screamed and closed her eyes. When she opened them, Rafik was leaning over her in real life, in Jerusalem, saying worriedly, "Are you okay? Or are you going bonkers, too?"

"What do you mean, 'too'?" Liyana's tongue felt thick after her brief, busy nap. "Who else has gone bonkers? Do you know what I dreamed? Remember that hill in front of the museum?"

Rafik's main interest was, who had pushed her? Had the horse statue reared up completely off its base and given her a kick?

He yawned. Then he said, "I'm surprised I still feel exactly like myself, you know what I mean? I thought when I got to the other side of the world, I might feel like somebody different."

$\mathcal{T}$O THE VILLAGE

*Think of all the towns and cities
we've never seen or imagined.*

Despite Rafik's questionable health, the family talked Poppy into traveling out to the village that very first night. They were insistent with him at the tea party downstairs. *Dinner is ready. You must come. The lamb is killed in your honor.*

Everything was decided, mysteriously, without anyone really saying yes or no. They crowded downstairs in a flurry to hail a whole herd of taxis and head north. Sitti rode in the car with the Abbouds, jammed up body to body with Poppy in the front seat beside the driver. Sitti muttered and patted him. It was the first time Liyana had ever pictured Poppy as the *son,* with his own mother bossing him around. Liyana, Rafik, and their mother crowded together in back.

The taxi veered wildly around a corner, then chugged slowly north on the road from Jerusalem to Ramallah. Poppy pointed out landmarks to them. *There's the garden where we had a party when I graduated from high school. Red lanterns were strung*

*from ropes. There's the shop of the shoemaker Abdul
Rahman—he's been inside hammering soles since I was
born.*

Liyana's eyes swirled with stone buildings, TV
antennas, metal grillwork over windows instead of
screens, flapping white sheets strung from
clotheslines right on the flat roofs of houses, signs
in Arabic, Hebrew, and English, and lumbering
buses. Rafik had gone to sleep again with his head
back against the seat. Liyana felt like poking him
to wake him up.

"It's not how I pictured it. What about you?"
her mother said.

Liyana answered softly, "Nothing is ever as I
picture it."

Had she thought Jerusalem would have a halo?
She certainly didn't think about—diesel exhaust.
They passed the military checkpoint surrounded
by striped orange sawhorses. In the bustling Arab
town of Ramallah, everyone walked around carrying
large mesh shopping bags. A man with a tray of
round flat breads stacked sky-high grinned at Liyana
through the car window when their eyes met.

Then the taxi headed into the rural West Bank
of orchards and tiny villages, each with its own
minaret and perched houses. Liyana said, "It's
gorgeous here!" and breathed deeply. She was also
thinking, "It's strange," but she was looking for

the silver lining. The dusky green of olive trees planted in terraced rows up hillsides, walls of carefully stacked stones, old wells with real wooden buckets.... Ancient men wearing white headdresses leaned on canes talking in slow time as the train of taxis, driving faster now, flew by into another dimension.

When the cars climbed the steep hill into the village, children popped out of front doors to look at them, as if cars didn't drive up there very often. Rafik sat bolt upright and Liyana said, "We're on the moon." Every house was made of golden or white chunky stone.

The moment they piled out of their seats, they were surrounded by relatives kissing their cheeks again. Liyana's face was starting to feel rubbed *raw*. A bearded man in a long cloak, whom Poppy introduced as Tayeb the Elder, shot a gun off into the air like a military salute. Poppy begged him to stop. What if the bullets came down on their heads?

Inside Sitti's arched main room, they sat on flowery gingham mattresses arranged in a circle on the floor. Liyana sat between Rafik and a shy girl cousin named Dina who kept smiling at her. An old picture of Poppy before he came to the United States hung high and crookedly on one wall. Liyana wanted to take a broom handle and straighten it.

"We're here!" Poppy kept announcing in English, then Arabic, like some kind of television host, and everyone would cheer. And a strange cloud passed through Liyana—they were *here*, but no one really knew her here, no one knew what she liked, or who her friends had been, or how funny she could be if she had any idea what was going on. She would have to start from scratch.

Poppy and Mom—whom everyone had started calling Soo-Sun, in a way that made her common American name sound almost Chinese—began distributing presents to everybody. They passed out boxes of heart-shaped soaps, fuzzy slippers, creamy pink lotions, fancy hand towels, men's shiny ties, and chocolates, which surprised Liyana, since they'd barely eaten chocolate in their own house. Mom had scurried around St. Louis buying these things before they left.

Everyone looked very hopeful. After they received their gifts, they compared them. Liyana produced ten pairs of earrings she'd bought for a dollar each for her girl cousins. Dina, amazingly, had tears in her eyes as she selected her pair. Rafik offered up—reluctantly, Liyana thought—a few packages of small cars to the boys.

Then the whole gigantic family sat around forever, visiting, waiting for dinner to appear. What Liyana would discover was this was positively everyone's favorite thing to do here—*sit in a circle and talk talk talk*. Poppy had told her they liked to talk about—everyone else. They watched each other with their hundred deep eyes. When Cousin Fayed and his family poked their heads through the door, or Cousin Fowzi and Aunt Muna entered with welcomes and a basket of oranges, everyone stood up, hugged, kissed, exclaimed, patted, and went through the entire cycle again.

"I think I'm getting hypnotized," Rafik said.

Then Aunt Saba, which Poppy said meant "morning," appeared carrying a large brass tray filled with steaming glasses of musky-smelling tea—*maramia*—an herb good for the stomach. Rafik drank five glasses. Back home he could drink a whole bottle of cranberry juice by himself at one sitting.

The grocer showed up, and the postmaster, and the principal of the village school, and the neighbor, Abu Mahmoud, who grew famous green beans, and all of their wives and babies and teenagers and cats.

But the extra visitors left just as a huge tray of dinner appeared, hunks of baked lamb surrounded by rice and pine nuts. The remaining family members gathered around to dig into it with their forks. Poppy asked if his family could have individual plates since they weren't used to eating communally.

Aunt Amal brought out four plates of different sizes and colors. Liyana's was blue, with a crack. Her aunt looked worried, as if she might not like it. Liyana ate a mound of rice and onions and sizzled pine nuts, but steered clear of the lamb.

Sitti kept urging Liyana, through Poppy, "Eat the lamb." She said Liyana *needed it.* Poppy told her Liyana was a very light eater, a big lie of course, but convenient for the moment. Rafik was drinking soupy yogurt, one of his two thousand favorite food items. "I'm recovering," he whispered to Liyana. "I'm feeling better now. Who is that guy and why does he keep waving at me with his ball?"

Rafik and their animated cousin Muhammad stepped into Sitti's courtyard to play catch in the glow from a single bright bulb, but Liyana felt too tired, suddenly, to follow them. Sitti asked Poppy some questions about Liyana—Liyana could tell because they both stared at her as they talked. Now and then her name cropped up in their Arabic like a little window. But she couldn't see through it. She thought she could close her eyes and sleep for two days. Even her watch felt heavy on her arm. It was 10 P.M. She hadn't taken it off since they left Missouri—how many time zones had they crossed by now?

Liyana tried to be polite to everyone by smiling

and tipping her head over to one side so they couldn't tell if she were saying no or yes. How long would it take till they knew one true thing about her?

Voices in the village streets bounced off stone walls. They rose into the night sky like kites, billowed, and disappeared. A *muezzin* gave the last call to prayer of the day over a loudspeaker from the nearby mosque and all the relatives rose up in unison and turned their backs on Liyana's family. They unrolled small blue prayer rugs from a shelf, then knelt, stood, and knelt again, touching foreheads to the ground, saying their prayers in low voices. They didn't mind that Liyana's family was sitting there staring at them. When they were done, they rolled up the rugs and returned to sit in the circle.

"Poppy," Liyana whispered, touching his hand. "Did you ever pray the way they pray?"

"Always—in my heart."

Sitti told Poppy she was going to make a pilgrimage to Mecca this year for sure, especially if he would give her money to ride the bus. Tayeb the Elder asked for money to install a shower in his new bathroom and Uncle Hamza said he could really use a stove and suddenly everyone was asking for things, voices tangling together as Poppy translated. He looked more and more uncomfortable.

Soon he turned toward their mother, saying, "When the talk gets to money, we get rolling," and he stood up.

He said they were so exhausted their heads were falling off. They needed to return to Jerusalem to their hotel immediately. Some angry grumbling erupted because the older relatives thought they should be sleeping in the village with their family, not in a hotel. Liyana felt the weight of centuries pressing her into a small ball. A yawn rose up in her so large she could not hold it back.

Sitti stood beside Liyana. They were exactly the same height. Sitti took both Liyana's hands in her own. She said, through Poppy, "I hope you will come back tomorrow and stay for many many days." Sitti said they would teach her how to sew and pick lentils and marinate olives and carry water from the spring on her head and speak Arabic. Poppy said, "She'll also teach you how to give a weather report by standing on the roof and licking one finger and holding it up in the wind." Everyone laughed when he translated this. Was it a joke? Were they making fun of her?

Sitti moved her hands around when she spoke, letting them weave and dance in the air. She lifted the tip of Liyana's braid to look at it. She kissed her twice on each cheek. And she pressed Liyana's face into her smoky scarf.

Outside, the sky felt deep and dark as if a large soft blanket had been thrown over the hills and valleys. They stood for a long moment with their suddenly huge family staring off across shadowy fields and orchards, smelling the turned soil and the sweet night breeze. A donkey hee-hawed somewhere, the sound echoed, and a car motor cut off so the silence seemed deep as the sea. Poppy took a deep breath. "Home," he said, and nodded at Liyana. He had his arm around her.

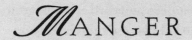

ℳANGER

She did not want her head
to be filled with large wishes and worries.

The Abbouds began looking for a house near Jerusalem and everything was either too big, too expensive, too little, too crumbling, too noisy, or too strange. One elegant house faced a billboard advertising "The Museum of Jewish Hatred." Poppy told the realtor soberly that he was sorry, but he couldn't bear to look out his window at that depressing sign.

Waves of sadness swept over Liyana unexpect-edly every time they entered a house that *might* become theirs and left it again. She thought of their neat white house with green shutters in St. Louis. She thought of their wooden screen door banging on its hinge. They kept passing the road sign TO BETHLEHEM and Liyana found herself singing, "O Little Town of Bethlehem" and "Away in a Manger" till Rafik covered his ears.

Each night, she added to her sack of dirty laundry at the hotel, refolding any clothes she could stand to wear another day in a stack on top of her open suitcase. Poppy asked, "Didn't you bring *anything* but that black T-shirt?" Only one of her suitcases had been sprung open so far. She wanted to be surprised later to find more familiar clothes and treasures waiting in her bags.

Rafik, however, had opened every case he brought and was living in a heap of toys and treasures, a neon battery-powered yo-yo, a skunk puppet, and a harmonica. He even had the group picture of his last year's school class standing up on his bedside table.

Liyana wished Uncle Zaki, Poppy's elder brother, had not asked "for her hand" for his son on their second trip to the village. Poppy got so furious, he actually hissed, and translated his answer for them later. "We do not embrace such archaic customs, and furthermore, does she look ready to be married? She is fourteen years old." In the village everyone seemed to be staring at her now as if she were an exotic animal in a zoo. She felt awkward around her relatives, as if they had more in mind for her than she could ever have dreamed.

She wished she had not heard that an Arab boy who was found kissing a girl in the alley behind her house got beaten up by the girl's brothers. What was wrong with kissing? Everybody else kissed *constantly* over here—but on both cheeks, not on the mouth. Had people reverted to the

Stone Age just because everything in Jerusalem was *made* of stone?

Poppy sat Liyana down on the hotel room couch, which they were growing quite familiar with.

"You are missing the point," he said, "if you imagine you can measure one country's customs by another's. Public kissing—I mean, kissing on the mouth, like romantic kissing—is *not okay* here. It is simply not done. Anyway, it is not *supposed* to be done."

"Not by anyone?" she asked. "Not by Greeks or Jews or Armenians, or only not by Arabs?"

With her luck she had been born into the only nonkissing culture, just when it started feeling like a valuable activity.

"I cannot speak for Greeks and Jews and Armenians. I used to trade desserts with them, but I cannot speak for them regarding kissing. Somehow I do not think they are as strict about kissing as the Arabs are. Probably to their benefit. Of course anyone can kiss once they are married."

Poppy looked suddenly alarmed. "Is there someone you want to kiss?"

"Oh sure, I just arrived nine days ago and I've already staked him out."

"Liyana, you must be patient. Cultural differences aren't learned or understood immediately. Most importantly, you must abide by the guidelines where you are living. This is common sense. It will protect you. You know that phrase you always hated—*When in Rome, do as the Romans do?* You must remember, *you are not in the United States.*"

As if he had to remind her.

When she went to bed that night, she pressed her face into the puffy cotton pillow. It smelled very different from the pillows in their St. Louis house, which smelled more like fresh air, like a good loose breeze. This pillow smelled like long lonely years full of bleach.

———

The next day Liyana's family rented the whole upstairs apartment of a large white stone house out in the countryside, halfway between Jerusalem and the town of Ramallah. A bus stopped right in front.

Surrounded by stony fields, the house had a good flat roof they'd be able to read their books on, if they spread out blankets. Poppy pointed out the old refugee camp down the smaller road behind the house—it had been one of the first ones from 1948. From the roof it looked like a colorful village of small buildings crowded close together. "Believe me," Poppy said, "it looks better from a distance. Camps are difficult places." Beyond it sat the abandoned Jerusalem airport—a few streaks of gray runway and a small tower. "It's fast asleep," Poppy said sadly.

Each wide-open empty bedroom in the house had a whole wall of built-in wooden cupboards and closets and a private sunporch. Finally they'd be able to unpack.

Their new landlord, Abu Janan, which meant the Father of Janan, looked like the Prophet of Gloom, with a huge stomach too big for his pants. He told them they probably wouldn't be able to get a telephone hookup for at least a year, since he just got his after requesting it forever.

Poppy said, "Well, I'll work on it immediately since I'm a doctor and require one. Also" (he winked at Liyana), "don't teenagers need to have telephones?" As if she had anyone to call.

"Where is Janan?" she asked.

"Who?" Poppy said.

"The person this man is the father of."

"In Chicago. Grown up."

Too bad. She'd thought she might have a built-in friend.

From the immaculate bare kitchen of their new flat, Rafik and Liyana could hear squawking rising from the backyard. They went downstairs and stepped outside to find a pen of plump black chickens pecking heartily in straw. A short cottage held their laying nests.

"We're living at a manger after all," Rafik whispered. "You want to sneak down sometimes and give them treats?"

"What is a treat to a chicken?"

"Cantaloupe seeds and the middles of squash."

"How do *you* know?"

Rafik shrugged. "I have many secrets. We could let them out someday!" The yard was surrounded by a wall so they wouldn't be able to go far.

Liyana felt a pleasant mischief lay its cool hand on her head again.

Rafik said, "Did you see that landlord of ours? He could use some exercise! If he chases them, he'll get some!"

Liyana mused. "Shouldn't we wait at least a week? Let's establish ourselves as law-abiding lodgers first."

"Then?"

A bus kicked up dust on the road after letting off a crowd of passengers. Their new neighbors who didn't yet know they existed.

"Then we have fun."

INTERIOR DECORATORS

*My father once said he'd like to paint
every board of our house a different color.*

Rafik tacked up bright travel posters from Poppy's travel-agency friend on the freshly painted white walls of his room. He posted "New York" and "Portugal," though he'd never been there, and "The Doors of Jerusalem" and "TEXAS USA," the place he hoped to go someday.

Liyana said, "Did you get any for me?"

Rafik said she could have "Lufthansa" but she didn't want it. She'd never even flown on that airline.

In St. Louis, Liyana's room had been painted a deep, delicious color called "Raisin." Her walls looked like an art gallery arranged with block prints and dreamy watercolors by her friends. She had a bulletin board with silly pictures taken at people's birthday parties and dried flowers and pages ripped from magazines that were too nice to throw away. The gleaming, golden eyes of a cat stared right at her in bed. She had a framed pastel portrait her mother had sketched of her when she was two and fell asleep on the blue rug in the living room. Liyana loved it very much and would have brought it to Jerusalem, but she worried the glass in the frame might break. She didn't bring Peachy's needlepoint alphabet or her personal portrait of Peter Pan, either.

Liyana thought she'd try living with blank walls for a month or two.

It was just an experiment.

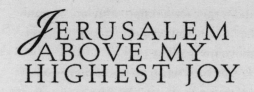

JERUSALEM ABOVE MY HIGHEST JOY

The city was a cake made of layers of time.

"I'm not going," Liyana told Poppy.

They were talking about Sitti's invitation to come out to the village so she could "teach her things" on weekends.

"Why doesn't she want to teach Rafik things, too?"

"Because she's a woman and she knows womanly things."

"She can keep them."

Poppy sighed, "Fifty years from now you will deeply regret this moment." He turned and stalked down the hallway toward his own bedroom. That's what he always said. *Fifty years from now I'm going to be very busy,* Liyana thought.

A few days before, Poppy had actually thumbed through a Bible looking for a quote he liked from the Psalms: "If I forget thee, O Jerusalem, may my right hand forget its cunning. May my tongue cleave to the roof of my mouth, if I do not set Jerusalem above my highest joy."

It made Liyana mad when he read it to her. Was there an underlying meaning? Was he saying she wasn't acting happy enough to be here? She wasn't in the mood to go shopping day after day to replenish their household supplies. She didn't even act excited about their new white Toyota, which smelled like fresh carpet and roses inside. "We could drive to Damascus or Aleppo!" Poppy said, standing back proudly to admire his purchase. "Well, we might have trouble getting across the border...."

Mostly they would just be driving back and forth from Jerusalem to Ramallah to their house, which sat so neatly in between.

Every morning at breakfast, when Poppy greeted Rafik and Liyana with his characteristic, "Good *morning!* And how are *you* today?" she felt like answering in a gloomier way. *I'm fair. I'm floundering. I'm lonesome.* Liyana begged Poppy to pass by their new post office box often to see if she had received any letters from home. *What was wrong with Claire?* She imagined Poppy watched her from the corner of his eye.

The Abbouds spent an entire exhausting weekend sightseeing nonstop around Jerusalem morning till night. Poppy wanted them to "get the lay of the land."

He led them up winding alleyways and down ancient stairs to the Church of the Holy Sepulcher he'd been telling them about for years. The priests here were famous for arguing to get the best altars for their own services. Poppy had done his homework on the wall outside the door when he was a boy and once saw two priests have a fistfight, rolling in the dust.

The dim Chapel of Calvary held a mournful mural of Jesus lying arms outspread and dead on the cross after it was taken down and laid on the ground. Mary Magdalene pressed her head to his feet. Mrs. Abboud cried when she saw it. At the Garden of Gethsemane, she cried again. Jerusalem was not exactly fun and games. Liyana's mother held a tissue to her eyes. "I'm just feeling very *moved* today, thinking of all Jesus went through—it's so haunting to stand on these same spots."

"There's always controversy, you know—which spot is the exact one," Poppy said.

"It's close enough for me," she said.

They walked along the crowded Via Dolorosa, where Jesus carried the cross and stopped at every station, so Mrs. Abboud could read aloud from her guidebook. German pilgrims, Italians humming hymns, and Japanese travelers wearing small purple caps converged on the same narrow pathways.

At the Wailing Wall, Jews in *yarmulkes* were tucking tiny notes and prayers into cracks between stones. Rafik wanted to know how long the notes stayed there. The most famous mosque of Jerusalem, the Dome of the Rock, gleamed golden against the sky.

The Abbouds trudged around the outside of the Old City while Poppy gave them a lesson in the gates—Damascus Gate, Herod's Gate, Jaffa Gate, the New Gate, the Lion's Gate (also known as St. Stephen's Gate), and—their favorite—the Dung Gate. Rafik and Liyana debated how the Dung Gate might have gotten its name.

They stopped at a hundred miniature stores with crooked floors so Poppy could greet the owners, kiss-kiss on both cheeks, introduce the family, and be offered coffee or tea, though he kept saying no. He said they had too many places to go to sit down anywhere.

"Everybody is a cousin of somebody and Poppy knows them all," Liyana sighed to Rafik.

"Yep," said Rafik, "but will you remember a single person you've seen? Good luck!"

Liyana knew she would remember sensitive-looking Bassam, who ran a spice shop, because he had a poster of the Hindu elephant-headed god Ganesha on the wall of his shop and that seemed a little—unusual—here.

Liyana and Rafik wanted to buy something from every food stand, but Poppy begged them to wait till their "very large and special lunch." As he greeted some ancient melon vendors who had known their grandfather, Liyana's eyes fell on a young man, who appeared to be a dwarf, weighing bananas on an old-fashioned hanging scale. He stood on a tall wooden crate behind his cart. His bananas were stubby and short themselves, more like exclamation points than parentheses.

He wore an orange stocking cap though the weather was warm. His tiny blue jeans must have been made for a boy. And his face looked as stony as the streets of the city—chiseled and sharply defined. He didn't smile even when he had three customers lined up. He just nodded and weighed their bananas. Liyana kept staring at him, the way she always picked one person in any crowd to stare at. She said to Rafik, "See that banana man? I'll remember *him*. On the day I see him smile, I'll buy a banana." Maybe he was sad because he was short, or he had wanted to do something else in his life.

"Where are the camels, anyway?" Rafik asked

Poppy. "I was hoping for camels." Poppy said they might see a few out in the desert toward Jericho, so immediately they begged him to take them there instead.

Liyana groaned, "Our feet are killing us. Also we're expiring from hunger. Isn't history better in small doses?"

"My precious children!" Poppy exclaimed.

They ate lunch in a famous underground Arabic restaurant, full of Oriental rugs, called *The Philadelphia.* Poppy gripped a waiter's wrist and introduced him around the table. "This young man's father," he said, "was the smartest student in my high school chemistry class!" Liyana noticed another handsome young waiter watching her as he rolled silverware into white linen napkins and stacked them in a mound. Did he wink? She thought he winked.

The owner, a nice man about Poppy's age, brought them steaming bowls of aromatic lentil soup, saying once they tasted it, they would keep coming back for more. The table filled up with olives, purple marinated turnips, plates of *baba ghanouj* and *hummus,* and hot flat breads, even before the real lunch came.

Liyana was feeling better by the minute. "With so much holiness bumping up against other holiness, doesn't it seem *strange* Jerusalem would have had so much fighting?" she said. Liyana was thinking of her teacher Mr. Hathaway back home, remembering the skeptical way he lifted one eyebrow any time she spoke.

"Think about dinner tables," her mother said.

"Huh?"

"How many fights there are in families, every day. People in families love each other, or want to love each other, but they fight anyway. With strangers you don't care so much. Think about it."

"Yeah," said Rafik, "if you didn't love someone, why would you even *bother* to fight with him?"

Poppy patted him. "My son, more a philosopher every day!"

"Do you think the Arabs and Jews secretly love one another?" Liyana asked.

"I think," Poppy said, "they are bonded for life. Whether they like it or not. Like that kind of glue that won't let go."

Two strong rays of light entered the subterranean restaurant through high-up windows along the street. One sunbeam fell directly onto the octagonal center design of a blue Oriental rug and the other lit up the red head of a very old lady. Poppy whispered, "See her hair? She dyes it with henna."

"That's what I'll do after I get my eagle tattoo," Rafik whispered.

"Being here with you all, I feel my heart has come back into my body." Poppy lifted a teacup and smiled.

———

Still, Liyana noticed Poppy didn't take them over to western Jewish Jerusalem for any kind of tour. He said he "didn't know it" and they might have to get a tour bus for that. The handsome waiter slipped a plate of *baklava* onto their table for dessert. They hadn't even ordered it.

THE PRINCIPAL WEARS A HAT POINTING TO THE MOON

Air was grinning around them.

Rafik was going to attend the Friends Girls School in Ramallah, even though he was a boy. The school accepted a few boys, too. It had been started by Quakers long ago and had a sunny campus with pots of geraniums lining the front steps.

Liyana's mother seemed happy because the schoolyard where Rafik would spend his recesses was surrounded by a high stone wall. She'd recently started talking about "safety" in a way that made Liyana jumpy. Liyana never thought about safety unless someone else brought it up. She didn't *want* to think about it, either. She wanted to live in an unlocked world.

Poppy and Mom did some research regarding Liyana's high school education and decided she might do best at an Armenian school called St. Tarkmanchatz deep in the Armenian district of the Old City.

The students there were trilingual, speaking

Arabic, Armenian, and English, three languages with completely different alphabets.

"Are the classes like a three-channel television set? What will I do when they're on the other channels? Will they think I'm a dunce for speaking only English?" Liyana asked Poppy. She was worried.

Liyana and Poppy went into town for the interview with the headmaster. They entered a huge iron door that led into the Armenian sector of the Old City and wandered the curling streets as if they were in a maze. The streets were unevenly paved and Liyana kept tripping. Poppy paused to gaze around them, saying, "I haven't been on these streets since I was a boy."

An old man sold roasted peanuts on a corner. When Poppy asked him in Arabic for the school, he pointed to an ancient building right ahead of them. The sign over the school's door was in Armenian—they could only read 1929.

Inside the main office sat a priest in a long burgundy robe wearing a giant pointed hat, or crown. Liyana wasn't sure what you would call the burgundy triangle sitting straight up on top of his head. Headgear? She tried not to stare at it.

He rose to shake hands, then waved them to sit on two rickety wooden chairs, speaking to Liyana in a careful, formal voice. "Do you know much about the Armenians?"

"I know they have a long and troubled history, like everyone else over here," Liyana said, equally carefully. "I know there was a terrible massacre of Armenian people, but I couldn't say the exact year. I'm sorry it happened."

"And you know that's why many in our community came to live in exile so far from our original homeland?"

She nodded. She was afraid he might ask her to say the Armenian alphabet or something, which she certainly didn't know.

A fan spun and a water cooler clicked. All the books on his shelf were in Armenian.

Then something wonderful occurred to Liyana.

"I love William Saroyan."

"Who?"

When she said, "The great Armenian-American writer who lived and wrote in California," he said, "Oh yes, oh yes!"

When Liyana was in seventh grade, her class had a story by Saroyan in their textbook. She looked up more of his works at the library and read "The Pomegranate Trees" out loud to Poppy. They laughed so hard, Poppy couldn't catch his breath. He lay down on the floor laughing, absolutely overcome. Later he said the wacky conversations in the story reminded him of his own family.

Liyana leaned toward the priest, suddenly

inspired. "I feel very close to what I know of Armenian culture through Saroyan's stories and look forward to learning even more."

That's when the air in the room changed. The priest leaned forward, too. His hat slipped a little. "So you are interested in our culture?"

"Absolutely."

Above their heads invisible angels started clapping.

The priest enrolled her, though she wasn't even one-fourth or one-eighth Armenian. He said she would be the only "outsider," a term that made her father flinch. Poppy spoke heartily, "Let's believe together in a world where no one is inside or outside, yes?" The priest didn't answer, but Liyana felt proud of Poppy for saying it.

Shaking hands again, the priest noticed the plain silver ring, her gift from Claire, on Liyana's finger and said, "I'm sorry, but you will note when you read our handbook that rings are not allowed in our school."

"Why is that?" Liyana asked.

"Distraction."

Poppy gave her side a meaningful poke that translated, "Ask no more."

Walking back through the narrow, winding streets to find their car, Poppy said, "Great idea you had, bringing up Saroyan."

Liyana said, "Distraction? If I were wearing a giant cosmic cone on my head, would I have room to talk?"

VERY VERY DISTANT RELATIVES

*"Genetics" means we have
the same little bowties in our blood.*

The beginning of school felt awkward for Liyana. She told her parents she didn't want to make any judgments till a month had passed. Liyana said to Rafik, "I would like to go to school with the donkeys in the field. To stand all day in the free air with an open mouth. No bells ringing."

Rafik shrugged and said, "Too bad for you. Maybe you'll like it soon." He said his school was a "piece of cake."

One day when Liyana returned from school by public bus, a lady she'd never seen before was sitting in their living room on the low couch. She rocked back and forth in her long, blue village dress, humming to herself.

Liyana nodded at her and went off to find her mother, who was in the bedroom digging through a box.

"Who's that lady in the living room?"

"I don't know. She showed up this morning and hasn't left. She doesn't speak a word of English. I kept hoping Poppy would come home for lunch today and help me out."

"Did you call him?" (Poppy had worked some magic with the phone company and gotten their phone installed within a week after all.)

"I did. He talked to her at length, but when I got back on, he said he hadn't the foggiest idea. She claimed to be his relative."

"So she's been sitting in there all day?"

"All day. I tried to feed her, but she waved the food away. I think she's shy."

"What are you looking for?"

"A packet of old pictures, the only ones Poppy has, to see if she might look through them and recognize people. Maybe that could give us a clue."

They found the pictures in a puffy envelope and the lady nodded for every one of them.

When Rafik came home after soccer practice, he said, "Who's that?"

"She's the sister of the Lost Pharoah," Liyana told him.

"Who's the Lost Pharoah?"

———

Rafik lit a stick of incense and wandered back and forth in the hall as if conducting a ritual. When

Poppy finally appeared, he sat with the woman and they talked a long time. She kept gesturing with her hands, but she didn't look upset.

In the kitchen Liyana washed spinach. Rafik had recently started cutting up onions, which their mother said was a great help to her. "That really irritates me," Liyana muttered, "that he does *one little thing* and you act so grateful. I do things every day!"

Poppy stepped in, shaking his head. "The woman's a mystery," he said. "I think she's a cousin of a cousin of a cousin who died before I was born and no one ever remembered to tell me about him. She lives in that little village on the lip of the mountain before you get to Nablus. I've hardly spent any time there, so I don't know any of the people she keeps mentioning."

"What does she want?"

"She wants me to buy her a dress."

"What?"

"It's an old custom. When someone returns from America, they buy every woman relative a bolt of cloth, for making a new dress. I guess it's to signify the success the traveler has had in America."

Liyana thought about the ten thousand relatives she'd met already.

"Everyone? Buy *everyone* dresses? Wouldn't that be impossible?"

"Of course. Especially if you had to buy them for people you'd never heard of before."

"So what are you going to do?"

"I'm going to drive her as far as Ramallah, where the fabric store is, and—I'll think of something. She can take the bus to her village from there."

They were breathing the rich scent of grilled onions and keeping dinner warm in the oven by the time he returned. "Well?" they all spoke at once.

He grinned. "I took her to the fabric store, all right. I told her to go ahead and get out. She thought I was going to park the car and come back and pick out a huge piece of red velvet for her. But instead I drove around the block and came straight home."

Rafik said, "You *dumped* her?"

Poppy shrugged. "The old customs have to be changed somehow, you know? Little by little. I told her I thought it was a stupid custom while we were still sitting here—but she was relentless. So—as easily as she appeared in our house, I disappeared. She'll get over it."

"Won't she be mad at you?"

"Have I ever seen her before? Do I live my life

82 *Naomi Shihab Nye*

being scared of the anger of people I don't even know? I am related to Hassan who is related to Hani who is related to Naimeh who is related to Fatwa who is related to this glass of water who is related to the river Jordan who is related to John the Baptist—come on!"

ℛEMEMBER ME

I'm the snip of red thread caught on a twig.

Maybe the hardest thing about moving overseas was being in a place where no one but your own family had any memory of you. It was like putting yourself back together with little pieces.

At home in St. Louis even the man at the grocery store remembered the day a very young Liyana poked a ripe peach too hard and her finger went inside it. She shrieked and the neighborhood ladies buying vegetables laughed. Forever after when she came into his store, the grocer would say, "Be careful with my plums! Don't get too close to my melons!"

It was a little thing, of course, but it helped her be *somebody*.

In Jerusalem she was just a blur going by in the streets. The half-American with the Arab eyes in the navy blue Armenian school uniform. Who?

PAST AND PRESENT ROLLED INTO ONE

Water came from the earth
and stories sprang from the stones.

Sitti kept Liyana's bed in the village ready, the pillow puffed. She pointed it out each time the Abbouds arrived for their regular weekend visit, but Liyana turned her face away. Why was it such a *big deal?* Sitti stroked her face saying, *"Ya Habibi, Habibti,"* cackling like a giddy munchkin.

But one Saturday morning, Liyana felt ready, as if a compass had swung round inside her and held. "I'll stay at the village," she said. She told Poppy and her mother that they could return on Sunday night and pick her up.

They'd be there all Saturday afternoon themselves, as usual, which relieved Liyana. If Poppy were with her, he could *explain*—who was who, what was what. It was all a guessing game without him.

Liyana put her backpack in Sitti's corner. She had brought a collection of poems in case she had time to read, and her writing notebook, and her small troll with rhinestone eyes. Sitti might like it. She could already tell Sitti got excited over very little things.

Rafik had disappeared with Muhammad again. Aunt Amal arrived to take Liyana's mother out to the orchards and show her the almonds and olives ripening on the branches. They carried baskets for picking herbs—oregano and mint, sumac and thyme.

Sitti motioned Liyana and Poppy toward the mounded oven called the *taboon,* large enough to step into, beside her house. She showed Liyana how to slap bread dough into flat rounds and fling them onto a hot black stone to cook. When her long dress flapped dangerously close to the flames, Liyana stooped to pull it back, but Poppy said, "She knows what she's doing." Their other relatives had modern electric bread ovens now, but Sitti refused to touch them. She remained devoted to the old ways of doing things.

She pitched Liyana another ball of dough, inviting her to try it. Liyana copied her motions, kneading, slapping, and swinging the dough high in the air as she'd seen pizza makers do in Italian restaurants back home. Sitti's loaves were perfectly round, but Liyana's bread looked like Australia. Sitti helped her shape and reroll.

By the time the hot breads were placed on a white cotton towel on the table to cool, Poppy had fallen asleep on top of Sitti's bed like a boy. Sitti leaned over him for a minute, as if she were examining her baby closely. Then she whispered to Liyana and gestured that they should leave him alone. Liyana was thinking, *So much for my translator.*

But it turned out she didn't need him so badly after all. Sitti lifted a tall clay jug onto her head and motioned Liyana to hike with her down the dirt road. They charged off into the breeze. Sitti kept glancing at Liyana's face as if to check on her. *Was she happy? Did she like this?* Sitti waved her arm at the expansive view across the valleys and hills. She blew a kiss to the air, which helped Liyana take a deeper breath herself. Liyana could skip if she wanted to. She could twirl in a circle with her arms out to feel dizzy.

No one watched them or acted formal. Liyana felt as invisible and happy as she used to feel coasting on her bike.

They passed the telephone operator's house and he waved at them through the open door. He had a switchboard in front of him with wires and holes, just like the switchboards in old American movies. They passed a few lone houses sitting off by themselves under gnarled trees. They passed a cemetery and Sitti turned her face away. Liyana noticed there were no words on any of the white gravestones.

Then they came to the spring, where water

gathered in a shining pool by the roadside. Sitti filled her hand and let Liyana drink from it. She'd never drunk from anybody else's hand before. The water tasted crisp. Then Sitti filled the jug slowly from a pipe jutting out of a ledge. Poppy had said the women still preferred this fresh "earth water" to the water that came from faucets. Sitti placed a thick cloth pad on her head and heaved the full jug back up there, to carry back to the house. Once the jug was in place, she balanced it without using her hands. She motioned to Liyana. *Did Liyana want to try carrying it?* Liyana jumped back. She couldn't even carry a peach on her head!

After delivering the water home and snapping green beans into a big pot to steam with a cinnamon stick, Sitti took Liyana to meet a neighbor who was stringing orange beads on nylon thread. The woman opened a cupboard to show Liyana dozens of lovely necklaces hanging on nails. She urged her to choose one. Liyana didn't wear necklaces herself, but selected a turquoise one strung with antique Palestinian coins. She could hide the necklace till her mother's birthday. The woman kept song sparrows in small wicker cages and gave Liyana two fat olive oil soaps to take home to her mother, too. She hugged Liyana good-bye.

Later Liyana realized how many things they had all communicated without trading any words.

Toward evening, when Rafik had returned sweaty from playing with his cousins in the fields and their mother had returned sunburned, happily stocked with a year's worth of herbs and some miniature embroideries to practice on, and Poppy had awakened from his second nap, they sat together on floor cushions by Sitti's bed cracking almonds into a wooden bowl. Liyana leaned against Sitti's shoulder so she could reach the bowl.

Sitti kept Poppy busy translating. She related her dreams as if they were news reports, staring into Liyana's face as Poppy spoke. "The other night I dreamed that a relative named Salim who died long ago came and asked me to accompany him to Mecca. I was so afraid. I want to go to Mecca, but not with somebody dead. I thought he would take me with him to the next world and make *me* die."

But then?

"When I woke up I saw that ugly cat sitting in my window, so I knew I was still alive."

Sitti popped two almonds into Rafik's mouth when he laughed and then she left the room to arrange the green beans and stuffed squash they were having for dinner on big trays.

Poppy leaned toward his family and said, "You'll notice Sitti's stories don't always hang together. She has no logical sense of cause and effect. Anyway, in this part of the world, the past and present are often rolled into one."

All the uncles were away at another village that day for a big meeting about land problems. The aunts had gone to Bethlehem to help a distant cousin prepare for her wedding. Liyana liked having fewer people around.

Poppy said he was afraid to buy Sitti a bus ticket for the pilgrimage to Mecca, because he really did think she might die soon afterward.

Why?

Sitti was back in the room by now, listening to them talk English and nodding her head. She said the squash would be cool enough to eat as soon as two birds crossed in the sky. Poppy didn't even blink. He just kept talking.

"Sometimes when a person looks forward to something for such a long time, it keeps them alive. Then when they accomplish it—*boom*." He studied such subjects. He said the old people he'd been seeing in the hospital here were incredibly "durable" for their advanced ages. "Lots of them are waiting for a true, independent Palestine, too. They're not going to give up when they're this close."

Sitti collected the almond shells in her skirt and went outside.

Liyana kept considering what Poppy said

about hopes being accomplished.

"Like you coming back to Jerusalem, Poppy?"

"I hope not."

———

At the last minute Liyana begged Rafik to spend the night in the village with her. He wouldn't care that he didn't have a toothbrush or change of clothes. "Listen," she hissed, "if I'm going to be out here pretending I understand what's going on, at least you could be with me." He agreed. He was really having fun here. The boys didn't do as many chores as the girls did, which irritated Liyana again. She felt like ordering them to go chop wood or mulch the trees.

Their parents left them after the big delicious dinner and two rounds of hot tea with mint and sugar. Sitti said she could read their fortunes in the tea leaves in the sugary bottoms of their cups. The tea leaves had their own alphabets and conveyed messages once the tea was gone.

Liyana felt so tired and chilly she wished she could curl up like a mouse in a hole. The minute the sun went down, the temperature in the stone rooms plummeted.

Rafik and Liyana looked hard at one another as the sound of their parents' car disappeared down the mountain. They were sleeping in the same room with Sitti, who took many minutes to unroll her gigantic pouchy belt, which doubled as a pocket. She emptied it of coins, a few crumpled money bills, a giant key, some loose buttons, and a pink comb, lining her treasures on a table. She wore her white pajamas under her clothes so she wasn't shy at all to slip her dress off right in front of them. Liyana took her own pajamas into the bathroom to change.

They slept on three skinny beds in a row, like in a dormitory. Sometimes Aunt Saba or Aunt Lena slept here, too. Sitti's bed had a big dent in the metal headboard. Poppy had asked her about it and she said the Israeli soldiers did it one day when they were in a bad mood.

Sitti muttered to herself after the lights were out.

"What is she saying?" Rafik whispered.

"You think I know?"

"Do you think she's praying?"

"No. It sounds more like a conversation."

"With who?"

"Did you know she believes in angels and dreams?"

Long silence.

He was fading, his voice slower.

"I hope—she doesn't dream—we're monsters."

MAD

What good is a mouth
if it won't open when you need it to?

Sometimes people carried anger around for years, in a secret box inside their bodies, and it grew tighter like a hardening knot. The problem with it getting tighter and smaller was that the people did, too, hiding it. Liyana had seen this happen, even in elementary school. Somebody wasn't fair to someone, and the hurt person just held it in. By the end of the year they had nearly disappeared.

But other people responded differently. They let their anger grow so large it ate them up—even their voices and laughter. And still they couldn't get rid of it. They forgot where it had come from. They tried to shake the anger loose, but no one liked them by now.

Liyana wondered if the person who could let it out, the same size it was to begin with, was luckiest.

In Jerusalem so much old anger floated around, echoed from fading graffiti, seeped out of cracks. Sometimes it bumped into new anger in the streets. The air felt stacked with weeping and raging and praying to God by all the different names.

———

One afternoon, Liyana walked over to Bassam's spice shop to buy coriander for her mother. She needed a purpose to start feeling at home. So she'd actually begged her mother for an errand. Bassam smiled to see Liyana again.

His shop was a flurry of good smells—jars, barrels, small mountains of spicy scent. Bassam weighed whatever you wanted on an antique scale that looked as if it came straight from the Bible. He put weights on one side of the scale and a large spoonful of coriander on the other. Then he poured it through a paper cone into a brown bag and folded the top over twice. He said, "So how are you doing over here? Are you finding your way?"

He gave her some fresh cardamom seeds still in their pods as a present.

She pointed at his elephant-god poster. "I read about Ganesha," she said.

He brightened and said, "He's my friend!"

They were talking about the Armenian sector and the best music stations on the radio when a Jewish man in a *yarmulke* walking by the shop addressed Liyana loudly in Hebrew.

Of course she didn't understand him. She

didn't even realize he was talking to *her*. But Bassam motioned to her to turn.

"What?" she said, and the man switched over to English.

"Why you bother with this animal?" he said, pointing to Bassam. "Be careful. Don't trust animals. Go to better stores in our part of town," so she knew he thought she was Jewish.

He probably didn't care that Bassam spoke very good English.

Liyana's legs started shaking. Her mouth opened wide and puffed out nothing. She felt feverish. She could have fainted on the ground.

The man said one more thing. "Be smart." Then he turned and walked away. Satisfied.

Later Liyana wished she had chased him through the streets and hit him with her little spice bag. She could have swung it into his face till coriander clouded up his eyes.

Bassam didn't say a word. He turned away and busied himself brushing spice crumbs off his table.

All the way home the words she hadn't said kept crying out inside her. "I'm an animal, too! Oh, I'm so proud to be an animal, too!"

She couldn't tell Poppy. She felt she had betrayed him.

What, she wondered, would Sitti have said?

Sitti might have howled like a coyote.

$\mathcal{R}$AFIK'S WISHES

He wished for a whole basket of
yellow pomelo fruits,
sweeter than grapefruits,
to eat by himself.

A German archaeologist was coming over for dinner. Rafik, starving as usual, flitted around their rooms saying, "I wish she'd hurry up. I wish I wish I wish."

"Bro, you're always wishing," Liyana said. She was reading about the old kings and queens of England for her history class. Now *there* was an unhappy group.

Rafik wished he could do his homework sitting straight up in the salt of the Dead Sea. He wished he could dig a hole so deep, he'd find a lost city. Or a scroll.

He wished someone would lower him into a well. When Poppy was a boy, he'd been lowered into a village well on ropes because his aunts and uncles wanted to know what was down there.

Inside the musty hole, Poppy discovered secret shelves and shallow corridors dug into its sides above the water level. He shone his light on ancient clay jars. Maybe they'd been lined up there from biblical times.

Poppy lifted out a deep blue vessel with a wide round mouth and a clay stopper. Small dried-up carob seeds rattled around inside.

Dozens of village people came by to see it that night. "How many jars are down there?" they asked him.

"Hundreds."

They had a town meeting about it. What should they do?

Poppy kept shivering inside. What if he had seen bones? Skeletons and skulls?

And why did the ancestors hide their jars inside a well, anyway? Maybe the jars were filled with precious oils back then. Maybe the well was a secret hiding place in case of invasion.

The villagers decided not to tell anybody. If they told, no telling what would happen—already the countryside teemed with jeeps and foreigners and curious expeditions.

Poppy said he could never look at a well in the same way again. He went back to his own family house in Jerusalem and started wondering what might be buried inside the *walls*.

All this made Rafik want to *discover* something.

"It's part of your heritage," Poppy told him. "Dig, dig, dig."

Finally the archaeologist appeared, smelling faintly of perspiration, and they dove into their cucumber-mint soup. She wore a khaki shirt and a gold neck-lace charm shaped like a shovel. She told about the project she'd been digging on for ten years, in the desert near Jericho. "It takes *patience*," she said, looking at Liyana as if she didn't have any. How did she know?

Rafik asked her if he could apply for a job.

She didn't laugh. She said he could come out on a holiday sometime and she'd find tasks for him to do. He could carry buckets or sift through shards. He could be an apprentice. Then Liyana started getting interested, too.

"Just today," the archaeologist said, "we uncovered a rich cache of pottery chips painted blue."

Liyana and Rafik stared at Poppy meaningfully.

Later, when the adults had a boring discussion about what was wrong with the world these days, Rafik wished they'd be quiet. He preferred talking about *bones*. He'd told Liyana that whenever adults started talking about "the world," the air grew heavy. Liyana was impressed with him sometimes. She agreed.

They wandered outside onto the balcony, just the two of them, and sat close together in the evening breeze facing west. Even though the Mediterranean loomed far out of sight, beyond hills, neighborhoods and coastal towns, Liyana imagined she could feel sea breezes brushing her face. Sometimes it seemed they were coming from another world.

"Do you like it here?" she asked Rafik.

To her greatest surprise, he answered, "Yes."

He hoped they would stay here forever.

He liked it so much more than he had expected to.

He didn't even miss playing baseball in the back lot anymore. Soccer was better. And he *certainly* didn't miss his piano lessons.

For the first time, Liyana felt totally alone.

$\mathcal{F}$RIENDS

How long does a friend take?

One afternoon Rafik was working on definitions for his English vocabulary list and asked Liyana, "When does a person go from being an *acquaintance* to a friend? Where is the line?"

Liyana said, "Hmmmm. The line. Well, do you have any what-you-would-call-friends here yet?"

He thought about it. "Sure. Well, maybe. This guy Ismael in my class is my friend already. I might have more than that. Don't you?"

Liyana said, "Hmmmmmm." He hated when she was in this mood.

Rafik persisted. "Could becoming a friend take just a few minutes? So someone would be your *acquaintance* very briefly? Or could you skip that step and go straight to friend? And can it go the other way, too? Like, can you be friends first, then become only acquaintances later? If you don't see each other anymore?"

Liyana wanted to think her friends back home would always be her friends. She said, "I think friendships are—irrevocable. Once you're friends you can't turn back."

"What's *irrevocable?* Another vocabulary word?"

———

Something bad was happening today. A chain of Israeli military tanks lumbered up the road. Liyana stared out the window glumly. "It looks ugly out there."

The silver-lining theory made her think they should do something to change the mood in the air. It wasn't hard to convince Rafik to drop his pencil. Having seen Imm Janan, their landlord's wife, take the bus toward Ramallah thirty minutes before, they went downstairs to their stony, grassless backyard and unhinged the door to the chicken coop for the first time. The chickens stepped out, at first tentatively, then wildly, as if they'd been loosed from prison. They flapped their wings up and down. The happy hens scrabbled in the dirt for bugs and worms. Were there worms here, like back home? Did the whole world have worms?

Liyana stooped to see a chicken gobble a plump green caterpillar. It wasn't long, thin, or brownish like an earthworm. Rafik interrupted her reverie by screaming, "It's leaving! One of the hens has flown away!"

The hens were so fat, Liyana felt astonished

they could fly. But one had indeed just taken off, over the whitewashed wall. Rafik and Liyana left the others, unlatched the gate, and went running after the vagrant.

Down the road, past the looming cedar trees that looked as if they might once have circled a cemetery, the chicken did a mixed fly-flap-and-skid routine. She bounced onto the earth, taking off again so quickly, they couldn't catch up with her. Rafik waved his arms as he ran. Liyana tried to keep up. "What will we do? She's too fast!"

They lost sight of her at the gate to the refugee camp. Liyana thought she had gone inside. "Oh no!" she wailed. "What if someone catches her and eats her?"

But Rafik thought she had passed the camp and was heading down through low bushes and scraggly trees toward the runways at the abandoned airport. "She thinks she's a jet plane!" he yelled. "She's taking off!"

Breathless, they ran around the perimeter of the airport, now strung with barbed-wire fences and signs that said No Entry in English, Arabic, and Hebrew. "Do you see her in there?" Liyana called. But they saw only cracked pavement and dust.

Would the chicken come home automatically at nightfall, like a homing pigeon or one of those movie dogs that walked a thousand miles by secret radar?

"What if the *other* chickens have flown over the fence by now and Imm Janan has returned and the soldiers are circling our yard?" Liyana asked.

Rafik said what Poppy always said. "You're a dramatist."

But then something great happened. Walking back toward home past the refugee camp, Liyana stared over the clutter of wires, posts, and sawhorses that made up its jagged boundary, and there, among clotheslines and ramshackle dwellings, she spotted one tall redheaded boy with their chicken cradled in his arms. He was petting it, his head down close to its face.

"Hey!" Liyana called. "Hello! *Marhaba!*"

The boy looked up and grinned. He called out something in Arabic that Liyana and Rafik couldn't understand. Then he walked out the front gate of the camp and said, shyly, "Hello? He is—your bird?"

"She," Rafik said. "She is—girl bird." Liyana couldn't imagine being technical at a moment like this. She felt so relieved to see the wayward chicken again that she put her hand out enthusiastically to shake the boy's free hand.

"Ana Liyana," she said, using the Arabic phrase for "I am Liyana" that pleased her, since it echoed so neatly.

The boy said, *"Ana Khaled."*

Rafik said, *"Ana Rafik."*

"You speak—Arabic?" Khaled asked.

Rafik answered, "Not yet. You speak English?"

Khaled said, "Maybe."

Liyana and Rafik laughed. Rafik asked, "What's *maybe* in Arabic?"

"*Yimkin.*"

A younger girl with puffy red curls similar to Khaled's ran up to them. She wore a loose pair of pants that looked like bloomers, and a pink T-shirt with Donald Duck on it. Khaled said, "This—Nadine. My—brother."

"No—your sister!" said Rafik.

The chicken was trying hard to get away again. One taste of freedom had inspired it. Khaled seemed happy to hand it to Liyana.

"You—tourist?"

"No," Liyana said. "We live in that house." She pointed up the road. "Can you come over sometime and visit us?"

Khaled looked at his sister, who looked hopeful. "You are—*Araby*?"

This gave Liyana a chance to say her favorite new Arabic phrase. "*Nos-nos.*" Which meant, half-half. Somehow it sounded better in Arabic.

Khaled and Nadine liked this a lot. They walked up the road with them, reaching over to pet the chicken as they went.

At the back gate to the house, they all shook

hands and laughed again. Nadine and Khaled pointed at the other chickens flapping around the yard and said, *"Alham'dul-Allah!"* which meant, Praise be to God!, and which Arab people used for nearly everything.

"Come back!" Rafik said to them. "Come over soon!"

After Liyana and Rafik had caught the rest of the chickens with great difficulty and latched them inside their pen, they dissolved in a flurry of giggles just as Imm Janan stepped off the bus out front with her loaded shopping bags. Liyana said to Rafik, "Khaled and Nadine. They're nice. Now you tell me. Are they acquaintances or friends?"

INVISIBLE

*Her mountain of notebooks hid
under four folded black sweaters.*

Since his childhood, Poppy had been wishing for a
hat that would make him invisible.

Where would he go if he had one? Where
would he travel?

"I would travel in and out of the rooms where
big decisions are made," he said very seriously. "I
would listen to things people say when they think
no outsider is listening. When they make decisions that will affect other people. I would be their
conscience, tugging at them quietly. And there
would have been peace in Jerusalem long ago."

Rafik said, "I would be like Superman. I would
fight crime and evil forces and no one would even
see me."

"It's a hat," Liyana told him. "It's not wings."

Their mother got all dreamy when Poppy said,
"*You* put the hat on now—where will you go?"
She would sit at the feet of great musicians and
opera singers as they practiced. She would soak up
their trills and scales, their perfect pitches. Or she

would ride around in Mother Teresa's pocket. She would shadow great saints and learn how to do selfless things for the world.

"Mom," Liyana said. "You're doing that already."

"No," she said, smiling. "I'm only doing it for you. I could do more."

What would Liyana do? She'd pop that invisible hat on her head, go to the airport, and get on a plane headed back to the United States. She would sit in First Class. She would curl up on somebody's food tray with the real silverware and the china plates.

Rafik said, "Let's hope the hat has shrinking powers, too, and makes you tiny, the size of a salt shaker. Otherwise that tray's going to *tip*."

Later Liyana would float around their old neighborhood, invisible as tree pollen, and see if anyone mentioned her.

Maybe she was completely forgotten.

She would drift in through Mrs. Mannino's window and hang suspended over the kitchen sink while she washed dishes. Liyana still remembered what Mrs. Mannino's coffee cups looked like, white with painted shafts of wheat tied together. She and Claire and Kelly Mannino drank spiced cider out of them.

She would fly into Peachy Helen's bedroom

where Peachy was buttoning her satiny housecoat, and whisper, "Lavender's blue, dilly-dilly, lavender's green." She'd click her invisible fingers, reciting rhymes Peachy taught her when she was very little. "Jack be nimble, Jack be quick, Jack jump over the candlestick." Where was Jack now? Was his candle all burned out?

$\mathcal{N}$O MORE MEAT

I will speak the language of animals
and wipe their blood from my teeth.

One day, when Poppy had taken the bus to work so Mrs. Abboud could pick up Rafik after soccer practice, Liyana rode along and they stopped first at a butcher shop to buy chicken for dinner. It was the first time Liyana had entered one here. She followed her mother into the stinky store crowded with stacked shelves of crooked stick and wire cages.

The chickens in the cages were alive and cramped, jabbering, in their boxy prisons. They were not headless body parts on Styrofoam plates wrapped neatly in anonymous plastic in a refrigerated grocery compartment. They were not thighs, drumsticks, and breasts.

Downy feathers from their soft chests stuck between the bars of the cages. Liyana pulled a feather free and smoothed her finger over it. The chickens were breathing, chattering, humming. They were *looking at her. At each other.* And lifting their wings.

Her mother took a deep breath and said,

"Wahad, min-fadlack." One, please. Poppy had taught her the necessary phrases to get through a day. She seemed to be avoiding eye contact with the chickens herself. The butcher would let you pick your own chicken if you wanted to, but Liyana's mother didn't.

Turning her back on the scene, Mom stared into the street as the butcher plunged his hand into a cage toward one very upset white chicken. Liyana didn't want to see any of it either, but she couldn't stop looking. He grabbed it roughly by its legs and it screamed. Then he swung it abruptly, upside down, so it went into shock and dangled limply a moment before he plopped it onto his bloody counter, grabbed the big knife, and slashed off its head.

Liyana couldn't help herself. "No!" She waved her arm as if to slap him.

Her mother gripped her shoulder. "Oh, stop."

Liyana's eyes filled up.

She had eaten chicken hundreds of times, but she had never witnessed this scene before. She thought, *It happens over and over and over.*

The chicken's body trembled and writhed after the head was severed, then fell still. The butcher turned to plunge the body into a steaming pot, then deftly stripped the feathers off, wrapping the body in white paper.

Did Liyana just imagine the other chickens grew much   quieter for a moment? That a sheen of horror hung in the air? Each time a new person stepped into the shop, the chickens must worry.

My turn.

People might say chickens couldn't worry, but something sensitive in their bodies must know.

At that moment, full of the rotten stench of the shop, Liyana's poor mother handing her money over to the butcher, not liking it either but saying *"Shookran,"* in a tight voice, Liyana became a vegetarian.

———

Her mother cooked the chicken's body with tarragon leaves that had traveled in a plastic bag all the way from St. Louis. She served the chicken's body over rice. Liyana took only rice.

"Why aren't you eating any?" Poppy asked.

Rafik shouted, "Liyana's on a diet! Someone told her she has pudgy cheeks!"

Liyana held her fork straight up like a scepter. "It's dead," she announced loudly. "And it didn't want to die."

RAFIK'S ESSAY ABOUT LIYANA

My sister is a very unusual person and I don't think she would mind to hear me call her that. She loves to read and walks around talking to herself. Or she can stay quiet for a really long time staring at something like an egg.

She has a very primitive hairdo and wears mostly the same three shirts and blue jeans or one skirt over and over. She says she will never cut her hair or wear makeup in her life and if I paid her one hundred dollars she wouldn't paint her fingernails red. Actually she looks younger than she is, which is almost fifteen.

She doesn't need lots of things to make her happy. In fact, money is one of her least favorite subjects. She says one thing she fears about growing older is that she will have to think about money and she doesn't want to. I told her I would be her banker. Personally I like to think a lot about cars, what features they offer and what they cost, but my sister will only talk about where they GO. She doesn't want to know anything else. I'm also better on the computer than she is, but we don't have one over here yet. Our father sold it when we moved. My sister does not want to know any of the fancy programs, she only wants to know HOW TO TYPE.

My sister and I don't fight much, but sometimes she gets mad at me like when we were still in St. Louis and I found this list she made called "Against Growing Up" that included things like "They forget what it felt like to see a rabbit for the first time" and "They are always busy and sticking to schedules." I stuck it on the refrigerator with a magnet where both our parents read it. They thought she meant them.

I probably shouldn't even talk about it now.

Rafik Abboud

TWENTY-NINTH DAY OF SCHOOL

*I wish I could press my mind
as flat and smooth as I press my shirt.*

"People talk about their first day of school or their last day, but they never talk about their twenty-ninth day," Liyana said to Rafik. They were sitting on the short wall in the backyard cracking pumpkin seeds between their teeth, tossing shells into the lilies.

Liyana had been counting. Her twenty-nine-day Armenian friends acted very kind to her. They seemed genuinely glad she was among them, as if grateful for a newcomer to liven things up. They liked it when she mimicked popular songs from the radio in the schoolyard. Liyana had never been shy to sing in front of people. Why was singing any more embarrassing than talking was?

She'd learned they were supposed to stand formally when a teacher entered the classroom. She tried clicking her heels together, like Dorothy in *The Wizard of Oz*. She learned that Armenian boys are dashing and have a mischievous glint in their eyes. A boy named Kevork said, "We heard Americans are wild. Are you wild?"

By the twenty-ninth day, Liyana's papers had proper headings, and her navy blue uniform had lost its bright gleam, its sharp pleat. She kept her silver ring in her pocket and slipped it on every day as she left school. On the twenty-ninth day, she forgot to remove it in the morning and the "directress" snapped at her as the girls stood in line for their "daily checkup."

On the twenty-ninth morning, the teacher called roll by last names only: Hagobian, Melosian, Tembeckjian, Yazarian, Zakarian. Liyana was last—*Abboud*—even though alphabetically she should have been first. She was the P.S. in the roll book. Her new friends added "ian" to her name to tease her.

On the twenty-ninth morning, her class discussed the isosceles triangle as if it had just been invented. Bahgen Bannayan got in trouble for not bringing in his history research on the Colossus of Rhodes for the third day in a row.

Mr. Bedrosian, the English teacher (though he liked his students to call him a "professor" as if they were in college), wore his gray suit, the only suit he seemed to have besides his black one. Small threads dangled from the hem and the buttons. He could use some mending. He spoke about William Blake and John Keats with *veneration* in his voice, though Liyana wished he would pick somebody a little more modern to talk about soon. Liyana wondered if he lived alone.

On the twenty-ninth day a funeral procession passed slowly beneath the open classroom windows. The students heard the low voices of the mourners growing louder and louder as they approached. Liyana didn't realize what the sound was at first since she'd never heard it before. Everyone in the classroom was silently reading. She stood to look out the windows and stared right down into the face of the first dead person she'd ever seen.

A woman's petite body wrapped in white was being carried in an open coffin high above the heads of the mourners. Her head looked small, precise, with pale wavy hair and closed eyes in purplish skin. Liyana felt magnetized. Had the dead woman studied geometry? Did she have a happy life?

Mr. Bedrosian said, "You will please take your seat, Miss Abboud."

By the twenty-ninth day, Liyana knew exactly where to go for lunch, either out into the sunny walled courtyard to buy sesame bread from the vendor with the huge tray on his head—she ate it with hard-boiled eggs and cheese and apples—or home with her new friends to eat their mothers' folded spinach pies. Here, in the slowest country on earth, the students had a whole hour-and-a-half lunch break.

Or Liyana could stroll by herself into the streets of old Jerusalem beyond the Armenian Quarter to walk among the shops. She pretended she lived in a different time. She squinted her eyes. She liked the *falafel* sandwiches at a place called Abu Musa's Falafel House.

On the twenty-ninth day, Liyana gave directions to French tourists. She carried an old lady's giant sack of onions up some steep and crooked steps.

On the twenty-ninth day she did something slightly bad. She didn't come back into school the minute the bell rang after their long lunch. She couldn't stop thinking about the dead woman. Had she died suddenly? There certainly were a lot of people in her funeral march.

Liyana lay on a low wall outside the school, her head swimming in a pool of sun, body hidden by a tangled vine from anyone who might approach. She thought, *How close this peaceful wall is every day while we are trapped inside.*

Voices from the classrooms reached across the hedge. Her Arabic teacher on the kindergarten floor hit a short stick on the back of a chair for rhythm, teaching the little ones another useless sentence. *Please hand me the bellows for my fire.* "And who has a bellows anymore?" Liyana wanted to shout. How many bellows would they ever have to ask for?

Liyana wanted to say useful things: *Tree, stump, soup, cloud.* She wanted to say, *No way! Let's get out of here!*

On the twenty-ninth day, she nodded an apology when she entered late. She could still feel the quiet leaves unfurling inside her mouth.

The kindergarten students stared at her in wonder when she appeared daily for fifty minutes after lunch and stuffed herself into one of their miniature wooden desks. All the little faces turned in her direction. She felt like a giant lost from her homeland. They wore white pinafores. Their cheeks were glowing and peachy. They must have thought she was a very slow learner.

Sometimes, when it was her turn to answer and she stayed silent, they whispered hints to help her. She couldn't even tell them how grateful she was. The teacher, who reeked of sour ash, rapped the tiny backs of his students' hands when they made a mistake. Their rosy faces puffed up with tears. He didn't hit Liyana, even after the twenty-ninth day's tardiness, though she made more mistakes than they did. Did he fear she'd knock him over backward? Well, she would.

Liyana had already started drafting a letter to the editor for the daily English/Arabic newspaper in Jerusalem, pronouncing such behavior primitive and unacceptable. Would the school expel her if it got printed?

On the twenty-ninth day of school Liyana decided she could forget about Jackson if Atom, the boy who sat across the aisle from her in regular class, smiled at her a little more.

WHAT YOU CAN BUY IN JERUSALEM

I keep my eye on
the mother-of-pearl dove earrings
in the shop window,
waiting for them to fly away.

You can buy gray Arabic notebooks with soft covers just the right size for folding once and sticking in your pocket. Liyana's class used them at school and she'd started using them for her own writings. She liked how the place for a "title" was on what English speakers would call the back. She even started writing in one back to front.

You can buy miniature Christmas cards that say "Flowers from the Holy Land" and include a flattened burst of wildflowers. The blue flowers turn out best, pressed.

Postcards show the Old City behind its golden wall and the inside of the Dome of the Rock through a fish-eye lens and the giant water jug at the Kfar Kana Church and the craggy olive trees in the Garden of Gethsemane and the mosaic floor of Hisham's

Palace. Liyana found some dusty black-and-white postcards at the American Colony Hotel gift shop that said "Palestine" instead of Israel and she bought them, too. They showed camels, steep cliffs, the skinny Jordan River, donkeys, and Bedouins in tents. A crooked sign on the stationery store said, SPECIAL BIG GOODIES SALE GOING FAST AND NOW.

You can buy glass vases handblown in Hebron and olive-wood rosaries and creamy white mother-of-pearl star pins and shiny brocade from big bolts of cloth at Bilal's Tailor Shop. You'd almost never see anyone in the United States wearing clothes made of such cloth unless it was a high-society person or a Barbie doll.

Liyana liked to finger the rich brocade. Bilal gave her scraps from the ends of bolts. She had red and purple, gold and silver. She was learning to sew small pillows at home. She made one for her troll. Poppy had gone to school with Bilal's father long ago, so Bilal told Liyana she could have his shop when she got older. He said he wasn't planning to get married or have any children.

Why not?

Because I'm too ugly.

He wasn't ugly.

Liyana stared at him when he wasn't looking.

You can buy millions of little decorated cups, with tiny saucers, for Arabic coffee and tea.

You can buy painted Palestinian plates and roasted chickpeas and olive oil soap made in Nablus with a red camel on the package and saffron, that spice that costs a lot of money in American grocery stores, very cheaply. You can also buy vials of holy oil and fancy jars of water from the River Jordan (stamped: **For External Use Only**, so you don't get carried away and drink it) that has a Certificate of Authenticity in Arabic, German, and English on the side of the box. It also says the Bishop of Jerusalem of the Arab Episcopal Church authorizes it. Liyana thought you were supposed to dab it on your temples if you were having an extremely hard day.

You can buy sweets and treats, gooey, sticky, honey-dipped, date-stuffed fabulous Arabic desserts on giant round silver trays. Some have layers of sweetened, toasted shredded wheat. Some are packed with white cheese or walnuts or pistachio nuts. The bakery shops have little low stools and low tables out in front of them. Liyana liked *katayef* best—a small, folded-over pancake stuffed with cinnamon and nuts and soaked in syrup. She took home three half-moons of *katayef* in a white cardboard box.

If you asked the price of anything, the shopkeeper would say, *"For you...."* and pretend he was giving you a great deal, but you knew he would say that for anybody.

$\mathcal{D}$ISPLAY

Is the whole world really looking?

Liyana combed her long wet hair out on the open front balcony of their house where the breeze smelled sweet as olive oil. Up the road, white sheets ballooned like parachutes from neighbors' rooftop clotheslines. She wondered if Jackson had kissed another girl in the same movie theater by now. She tried to remember the way his crisp shirt collar stood up against his neck. She wondered if Claire had a new best friend. Her recent letter, on a blue air-letter sheet, didn't say so. Far off, Liyana could see a girl with red hair running at the refugee camp, carrying something large in her arms. Was it Nadine? Then Poppy called her back inside.

"Please," he said urgently. "Don't be so public about it. You're making a *display*. Comb your hair in the bathroom. Comb it in your own bedroom! Don't do it out there where all the taxis and shepherds can see you."

Sometimes he sounded as if she were breaking his heart.

Liyana's father still talked about shepherds as if they were everywhere. Now and then an ancient shepherd in a dusty brown cloak would pass Sitti's house up in the village, tapping a wooden cane against the stones. He didn't even turn his head to notice Liyana and Rafik staring at him from the doorway. All he cared about were his goats and sheep with painted red or blue bottoms so he could find them if they got mixed up with other animals. Maybe his own dusty memories followed him up the path.

But Poppy acted as if their modern apartment on the Ramallah road was still surrounded by shepherds. Poppy saw what *used* to be there.

Maybe, Liyana thought, he's afraid a shepherd will fall in love with me and come ask for my hand. I will never *ever* give my hand away. Even the phrase disgusted her.

Sometimes she heard her father say, "We are *Americans*," to his relatives—when she walked the village streets alone just for exercise, pretending she was giving Jackson a tour, or when she flipped the round dial on Sitti's radio, or when she slouched in the corner of Sitti's room with a book in front of her face.

Americans?

Even Poppy, who was always an Arab before?

Of course there was never any question about

their mother being an American, but Rafik and Liyana walked a blurry line.

Liyana tipped from one side to the other.

The minute Poppy told her to stop combing her hair on the balcony, she toppled onto the American side, thinking, *If I were at home on a beach I could run up and down the sand with just a bathing suit on and no one would even notice me. I could wear my short shorts that I didn't bring and hold a boy's hand in the street without causing an earthquake. I could comb my wet hair in public for a hundred dumb years.*

$\mathscr{L}$IT UP

*She turned a corner
and everything changed.*

"You keep getting me in trouble," Liyana's friend Sylvie sighed on one of their lunchtime walks from school to the *falafel* stand. That morning Liyana had urged Sylvie to defy the "directress" who ordered her to remove a tortoise-shell clip from her hair. Liyana whispered, "This is getting ridiculous! Say no!" and Sylvie peeped, "No" in a thin voice that caused her to get a detention note. She would have to stay after school.

Sylvie pointed to the Armenian man with giant keys dangling from his belt who locked the door of the Armenian Quarter every night at 10 P.M. He opened it again at 6 A.M.

Sylvie said, "Last week, I was running up the street fast from a movie at the British Library. This man saw me coming, but the time on the clock was 10:01 and he locked the door right before I reached it. He would not let me come in! I had to walk to the house of my aunt in the new city to sleep—a long walk in the dark! My mother was so mad. She said I can't go to movies anymore."

Liyana marched up to the man and asked, "Why do you need to keep that door locked, anyway? No one *else's* neighborhood is locked."

He stared at her as if she were a thief digging for secrets. "Security," he said gruffly, and turned away. She hated that word. Now Sylvie was embarrassed and walking back to school early without her. Maybe it was an excuse. She still had some leftover homework to do.

Just outside the Quarter's huge door, on the path to Jaffa Gate, sat the Sandrouni family's famous ceramics shop. Poppy had pointed it out to Liyana as a landmark. The Sandrounis painted beautiful tiles, lamps, and bowls with blue interiors, and scenes of Jerusalem—domes, towers, and pointy trees.

Liyana, feeling suddenly bereft without her friend, saw a crowd of tourists heading in there, so she turned and followed them, as if she were part of their group. No one noticed her.

The tourists began buying like crazy. They pointed and flipped credit cards, speaking a language Liyana couldn't identify—Danish? Dutch?

Liyana's eyes fell upon a small, shapely green lamp, exactly the color of the green grass she missed back home in the United States—who ever thought about grass when you had it? Who ever thought about missing a *color*? The lamp would be perfect for reading in bed.

Then she looked at the price tag. She couldn't understand it because the writing was so fancy, like calligraphy. She motioned to a boy standing behind the counter with his arms folded, near the reams of tissue paper and stacks of cardboard boxes. He raised his eyebrows and walked over to her.

He smelled like cinnamon. Liyana thought he might be one or two years older than she was.

"Excuse me, how much does this cost? Can you read it?"

He stared at her school uniform, speaking English smoothly. "You are not—with them?"

He pointed to the group.

"I am not!"

"You are—with who?"

Then she felt like Crispin Crispian in that old children's book by Margaret Wise Brown, the dog who belonged to himself.

"I am with myself."

He smiled broadly. "I am also with myself," he said. "I like to be with—myself."

His hair rolled back cleanly as a wave at the beach.

"You do?"

"Almost always."

"You don't get tired of your own self?"

"Never."

"You don't get lonely for other people?"

He looked around the crowded shop. "How could I? Other people are everywhere."

They both laughed.

"Do you go to school?" Liyana asked him.

"Of course," he grinned. "I am a—scholar. I do my homework every day. But right now—I am—eating lunch."

"So am I!" she said. "I am eating lunch, too."

Neither of them had any food.

"By the way," he said, "I can't read this tag either."

He called over a member of the Sandrouni family, who quoted something equaling about sixty-five American dollars. Too much! Liyana still had to translate prices into dollars in her head for them to make sense to her.

"Thanks."

"Do you want it?" he asked her.

"Well, I want it—but I can't afford it. Maybe they'll have a sale."

The Sandrouni man placed his hand on the cinnamon boy's shoulder. "Has he been telling you stories? Has he promised to give all my precious cargoes away for half price?"

Liyana laughed and thanked them both and

stepped back outside toward Abu Musa's where little cakes of *falafel* were frying. Abu Musa slid her crispy planets of *falafel* into pockets of warm, fresh pita bread and Liyana bit down hard. She was starving.

That night at dinner she said, "Poppy, today I fell in love with a lamp."

INTERVIEWING SITTI

Prepare for an unexpected visitor heading toward your door.

Back in the United States, Liyana's classes had oral history assignments where they were supposed to go home and ask their oldest relatives or neighbors what the world was like long ago. *What did you eat? What did you do for recreation? How did your mother cure a headache?* They could write the answers down or tape them, then choose the most interesting parts and compose a paper.

Of course Liyana always picked Peachy Helen, but Peachy would protest. "Honey, you think I remember that far back? I barely remember what happened yesterday! Let's just forget about it and share some scones with lemon curd, what do you say?"

Liyana would open Peachy's dresser drawers, pulling out a silver bracelet engraved with tipis and canoes, and dusty powder puffs, trying to jar her memory.

Usually she'd end up having to talk to Frank,

their neighbor in blue overalls who specialized in car engines and organic farming methods. He didn't remember much about childhood, or he wouldn't tell. But Sitti *remembered everything*. She even remembered when a Turkish tribe rode south past Jerusalem and the children were told to lie down in ditches so they wouldn't be run over by horses.

The problem was Liyana could only have a deep conversation with Sitti if Poppy were present. In Arabic class at school, Liyana was just learning the colors—*fidda* for silver, *urjawaani* for purple.

Anyway, Sitti loved when Poppy was present. She rubbed the back of his hand till he looked uncomfortable. He had been her last of eight children, born when she was past the usual childbearing age.

One Saturday in the village, with a light rain falling softly outside, Liyana tested her cassette tape and plopped down on a floor mattress beside Sitti, who was cracking almonds again by her fire in the oil stove. Liyana slipped off her blue Birkenstocks. Sitti picked one up, turned it over, looked at its sole upside down and said in Arabic, "It's too fat."

Tell me a story.

"About what?" Sitti laughed. She offered

Liyana an apricot. *The whole world was a story. Stories were the only things that tied us to the ground!*

Because she knew Sitti liked the subject, Liyana asked for "a story about angels." Poppy looked dubious even as he translated. He thought angel talk was foolishness.

Sitti stared at Liyana's cassette recorder as if it were an animal that might bite her with its tiny teeth. A thread of faraway music floated past and vanished.

Sitti placed both hands over her own eyes, as if casting a spell on herself, and began speaking. "Your grandfather, my husband, who died so long ago already, used to come home with his pockets full of a plump kind of dates, not those thin, dried-up ones that make you thirsty even in your sleep. He would present them to me as if they were coins or golden bracelets. He knew I loved them very much. We would place them in a white bowl covered with a cloth in the cabinet and we would eat them one at a time and I am not ashamed to say we did not tell the children they were there. Because one hundred little children from everywhere were always passing through this house. And there would not have been enough of them to go around, you know? But also, we wanted them ourselves!" Sitti laughed her throaty laugh.

"So one day I was taking a nap as your grandfather traveled up to Galilee and an angel appeared in my dream and said she would give me some important advice, because she was an angel. 'How can I be sure of that?' I asked her. I can't believe I was so rude to an angel!

"She said, *I will soon appear to your husband, who is carrying luscious dates in his pockets and I will ask him to share them with me and he will not be able to say no. Check with him when he comes back. That will prove it. Now here's the advice*—and she gave it to me. So the minute he returned I said, 'Did you get dates?' and he looked sorrowful.

"'Yes,' he said, 'but as I was standing in the *souk*—the marketplace—a young girl with strange eyes came up to me and said, *Please sir, I beg you for the food you are carrying in your cloak,* and as she seemed to have some extra power to see through cloth, since the dates were not visible, I felt obliged to hand them over. Then I couldn't find any more to buy before I came home.'"

Liyana asked, "What was her advice?"

"What? Oh. Not to buy the cow. Someone was selling a cow just then. We never have many cows around here, you know. There's only one right now, down the road in Hossaini's courtyard. Most people like goat's milk better. But I always liked cow's milk better so I wanted your grandfather to buy a cow that was for sale in the next village. He didn't want to. He didn't like cow's milk. Also, cows need more to eat than goats. And he didn't want it tied up in our courtyard at night taking up all the room.

So we didn't buy it. Good thing! Because we heard it died only a few weeks later. So the angel saved us from trouble! And all we lost was—a few dates."

Sitti cleared her throat and smiled. She stared at Liyana meaningfully. Poppy was finishing his translation. He still looked dubious.

Leaning over to Liyana, Sitti stroked her hair, the way you'd pet a cat or dog. "Always listen to the angels who find you," she said. She placed two fingers in the center of Liyana's forehead and closed her eyes.

So Liyana closed hers, too.

Maybe this was a charm.

———

When Liyana's aunt had to go to the hospital because her legs swelled up, Sitti said they swelled "because she has such a big and heavy head."

When Poppy told her that had nothing to do with it, she said, "What do you know? Your head is normal sized."

If a bird pooped on a clean white sheet while flying over the clothesline, that meant bad luck.

But if it pooped on your head, that meant your first child would be a boy.

Sitti wouldn't wear socks because cold feet would help her live longer. She thought Liyana should stop wearing socks, but Liyana couldn't stand it.

Sitti perceived messages everywhere. *You will soon go on a long journey to a place hotter than this place. Beware of a bucket.*

Liyana liked this stuff. She made a whole new notebook for it.

Poppy said he became a doctor because he grew up with such superstitious people. "They drove me crazy," he told Liyana in private. "I had to balance them out."

"Do you believe in heaven?" Liyana asked Sitti on the day of their interview, and she answered quickly, "Of course. It's full of fresh fruit." They took a short break to slice three Jericho oranges in half and share them. Sitti closed her eyes when she swallowed. Then she bustled around the room, muttering, sweeping the windowsill with her short-handled broom, straightening the bags of rice and flour and sugar on her shelves. She pulled a few strands of long hair out of her pink comb.

"What's she saying now?" Liyana asked.

Poppy said, "I think she's reciting the bees passage from the Koran."

Liyana sang out, "Ho!" to get her attention again.

Sitti jumped. "Sit down!" Liyana begged her. "Please! *Min-fad-lick co'dy hone!*" It was one of the first phrases she'd learned.

Liyana asked Sitti to tell more about her dreams at night and she said, with a mournful expression, "I dream of all the hard times I had in this life. And how mean the Jewish soldiers act to us. They don't even know who we are! And I dream of the way I felt when my most beautiful and beloved son," she paused dramatically, staring at Poppy, "went so far away from me I couldn't even see the tip of his shadow."

Liyana's father liked this conversation less and less.

Sitti ordered Poppy to give money to the poor before she died and more money to the grave digger and the women who washed her body. She insisted the people who buried her should leave lots of space in her grave so she could sit up to talk to the angels. She didn't like to talk to anyone lying down.

Liyana laughed out loud, but Poppy stood up, rubbed his hands together over the fire, and said, "Let's do something else."

RAFIK'S ESSAY ON KHALED AND NADINE

We have some new friends who live at the refugee camp down the little road behind our house. They have a bicycle and we do not and sometimes they let us ride theirs. The tire is rubbing the fender. Poppy says we can get a bicycle soon. Liyana says she hopes we can get two. They caught our chicken when it flew away. It is not really ours but we act like it is. Khaled thinks we live in a very big house because their house has only two rooms. When we visit them, Nadine, his sister, makes us drink this red juice made from pomegranates which makes my mouth go into shock.

Sometimes they come over and watch Abu Janan's television with us. They don't have a television and we don't either. Abu Janan says it makes him happy when people fill up his rooms. Liyana likes ancient reruns of "I Love Lucy." She says Desi Arnaz and his cute accent remind her of Poppy. I like "Tarzan," who reminds me of Liyana. I wish Abu Janan had a Super Channel so we could pick up "Star Trek," my favorite American show. Liyana has no interest in "Star Trek" at all. She hates the jumpsuits the characters wear and says their faces have seams. Also she says she has never seen anything green on that show, like a blade of grass or a tree. So she is glad there is no Super Channel and when I told her I would save up my change from my lunches so I could pay for the channel, she said she would steal my money and donate it to the refugee camp.

Khaled and Nadine like anything at all. They have lived in the refugee camp all their lives. They like whatever we watch. They roll their Rs when they speak English and we told them they do not have to do that. I'm sure they could tell us a lot of things, too.

Rafik Abboud

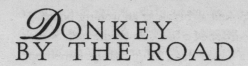DONKEY BY THE ROAD

*Emily Dickinson never had
to move across the sea.*

After a nurse appeared at St. Tarkmanchatz without warning and plunged a clumsy cholera injec-
tion into the arm of each student, Liyana stayed
home from school for days with a raging fever. "I
think she *gave* me cholera," Liyana mumbled, after
falling asleep with a thermometer in her mouth.
Her mother bathed her face with cool water and
set up a water pitcher beside her. Her father gave
her some medicine he worried wouldn't help
much. They both said, "Rest, rest, rest."

From her bed, she could hear her family continuing their lives without her. Clinking. Opening
doors. Rafik running water in the bathroom.

She was—*incidental*—to the planet's actions.

———

For one day she lay dreaming of the part in
Jackson's hair. When she had told him she was
leaving the country, a week after their kiss at the

movies, he looked as blank as an ironing board.

Someone dropped a book down the hall. Someone banged a locker door. Why did she remember those sounds?

He put on a cowboy voice and said, *"Well—see ya later—pardner."*

That is what he did.

———

The second day she lifted her hand to flip open a book of poems by Emily Dickinson, trying an experiment. Each time Liyana read a Dickinson line she really liked, she'd close her eyes and make up a line of her own inside her head. I'm not copying, she thought. I'm being *infused*. It's like drinking water straight from Sitti's spring.

When she read, *I felt a Cleaving in my Mind— As if my Brain had split*—her own head answered, *A Canyon opened—where before there had been smooth land. Now where do I stand?*

———

The third day Liyana was sick, she watched the sun crawl through her room as the hours progressed. It does this every day when I'm not here to watch it, she thought. Light rays crept across the windowsill, touching the legs of the table, and her schoolbooks toppled like monuments beside the tangled sheets of her bed—she'd kicked the blankets to the floor because she was SO HOT.

Long fingers of sun inched across her mattress. When she thought, this is the same sun that strokes the faces of my old friends back in my earlier world, her eyes felt thick. What was Claire doing at this moment? Claire's recent letter told about the school spelling bee that Liyana had won the year before, a new singer that everybody liked, crushes and anticrushes. It also said, "Are you *all right?*" because the bad news of Jerusalem made it across the ocean more quickly than good news ever could. If Liyana answered at this moment, she would have to say, "No."

Sitti appeared that afternoon with a flushed face, looking upset. She kept repeating something so Liyana's mother called Poppy at the hospital to translate. Poppy had spoken with Sitti that morning by telephone and mentioned Liyana was home sick. Sitti was furious he hadn't alerted her right away. Was he trying to insult her? Didn't he know she could make Liyana well?

Sitti closed the door of Liyana's room and smoothed the white sheets out on the bed, muttering the whole time. Sitti made Liyana lie very still with her arms stretched out alongside. Plucking a handful of silver straight pins from her plump cloth belt, she stuck them one by one, standing up, into the sheets around Liyana's body. Liyana kept cracking her eyes open to peek at what Sitti did. She mumbled the whole time she worked. More and more pins appeared. There must have been hundreds! Soon the pins outlined Liyana's body like a metallic running fence.

Then Sitti said a series of prayers. She leaned over Liyana with a rocking motion, back and forth, rubbing her own hands together over Liyana's body and opening them wide. She flicked her fingers, as if she were casting the illness aside. Liyana felt spellbound. A cool current seemed to shoot through the pins around her. Were they breaking the circuit of the fever or what? She couldn't even tell how long all this went on. Twenty minutes? An hour?

Rafik returned from school and stepped into Liyana's room to say hello to Sitti. "Wow!" he said. "It's a voodoo bed!" Khaled and Nadine were downstairs sending *Get Well* greetings.

Then Liyana began sweating profusely. Sitti acted happy now. She took towels, wiping Liyana's face and arms and legs very hard. Liyana called to her mother, "I'm *starving!*" It was the first appetite she'd had in days. Her mother brought her slices of fruit and toast and soup.

All through dinner, Rafik reported to his sister later, Sitti chastised Poppy for not having let her heal Liyana earlier. She shook her finger and frowned, telling him he should have been smarter, especially since he was a doctor and all. She slept on the couch, and left early the next day, on the first bus back to the village.

The fourth day Liyana felt well enough to eat three bowls of tapioca pudding. She could have written to Jackson to say, "Guess what? I forgot your last name."

Instead she stood by the front window staring down on streams of cars passing by. A yellow license plate meant Jews and blue meant Arabs. When you stayed home for days in a row, it seemed strange to remember all the places you would have been going otherwise.

Liyana could see the old man, Abu Hamra, pushing his cart of lettuces and cabbages up to the crossroads where he sat with it. Abu Hamra didn't like you to peel back the outer layer of a cabbage to peek inside. The first time Liyana visited his stand with her mother, she idly tried to see inside a tight cabbage's head, but Abu Hamra snapped at her so loudly, she dropped it.

Poppy said Abu Hamra's family had their well closed in by Israeli soldiers a few years ago after his nephew was suspected of throwing stones at an Israeli tank. That could make you mad for a long time, Poppy said. Losing your water because of a rumor.

Beyond the lettuce cart, a donkey sprawled by the road on his side, head down, as if he were sick, too. Where had he come from? Had a car hit him in the night? No one stopped, or paid him any attention.

Liyana slowly pulled on her oldest, palest blue jeans. She hadn't been dressed in four days. She never knew blue jeans were so heavy. Her mother stood in the kitchen chopping vegetables for soup. The house smelled healthy, of celery and carrot broth. Her mother looked surprised to see Liyana up and about.

"Are you well?"

"Not quite, but I'm going down to see the donkey by the road. I think he's hurt or sick."

Her mother shook her head. "The fever must have affected your brain. No ma'am. Get back in bed, dearie."

For some reason Liyana started crying.

"He needs me," she moaned. Then, more logically, "What if he needs me?" She begged her mother to let her carry him a pan of water.

Mom examined her with a tipped eye. Then she dried her hands thoroughly on her apron. "I'll go with you," she said. "Put a sweater on, too. It's windy out."

They filled the bottom of the steamer pan with water and took along a saucer and spoon.

The donkey's velvety eyes were closed. He

breathed heavily and seemed to like their gentle stroking. His muscles relaxed. A man in a car slowed down and called out to them in Arabic. Liyana shook her head.

"I think he said the donkey's dead, but he's wrong," she told her mother.

"Is your Arabic really that good already?"

"No, but I have a better imagination in Arabic now."

The donkey opened one glossy eye to look at them, but stayed down.

They spoke soothingly to him, spooning water onto his dry tongue. He licked it slowly around inside his mouth and swallowed. "Sweet donkey, take it easy, have a little sip."

Liyana's favorite Christmas song had always been "The Friendly Beasts." In one verse a donkey speaks: *I, said the donkey, shaggy and brown, I carried His mother up hill and down, I carried her safely to Bethlehem town, I, said the donkey, shaggy and brown.*

Liyana asked her mother, "Do they have a humane society here?" Her mother didn't know. While they discussed it, the donkey opened both eyes together for the first time, stared at them, heaved his deepest breath yet, and died. He was suddenly, absolutely gone. They didn't see any soul rise out of his mouth or nose, though they were looking hard.

For the second time in an hour, Liyana cried. Even her mother was wiping her eyes. Where had he come from? She would ask Khaled and Nadine if someone was missing a donkey from the refugee camp. Liyana wanted to bring a sheet out from the house to cover him, but they only owned the sheets for their beds and one set extra. Her mother put a soft hand on Liyana's shoulder.

"Let's go on home," she said. "We did what we could. And we were with him when he left us."

In the night his body disappeared. Maybe someone with a truck carried him away. Liyana felt bad that nobody stayed with him till that happened.

———

The fifth and last day that Liyana was at home recovering, she thought about donkeyness all day. She tried to sketch a donkey in her notebook. Her drawing was hopeless. Some people say a donkey is a "humble" beast—unlike a proud Arabian horse, for example. She thought about the word "humble" because Poppy had told her it was something she needed to work on.

She did not feel humble. She didn't think she was *brilliant* or anything, but she *did* want people to like and miss her. She wanted more letters stacking up in Postal Box Number 898 that said,

"Nothing is the same without you" and "Please come home soon." She pretended they were on their way. Poppy would flip them out of his brief-case and say, "Jackpot!"

Then she thought about the boy she'd seen in the lamp store. His dark hair combed smoothly straight back.

They could meet again. It was a small enough city.

DETECTIVE WORK

*We used to leave notes
on smokers' doorsteps saying,
"Excuse me, but did you know your lung cells are
shriveling up?"
Signed, The F.B.I.*

Liyana began visiting the Sandrounis' ceramics shop every other day, memorizing the intricate curls of vines on fancy tiles.

She pretended she had various missions: to collect the store's business cards to send to her friends back home, whose mothers had enormous interest in painted ceramics, or to purchase a small blue drinking cup, or to check again on the price of that green lamp which she would really love to see sitting by her bed. She wouldn't even mind learning how to electrify things. She studied cords and switches.

The Sandrounis soon greeted her as if she were their old friend.

"Ho—back again? We are irresistible!"

Mr. Sandrouni folded a newspaper he was reading very carefully. "You know what?" he said to

Liyana, who just happened to be standing nearer to him than anyone else. "I think it is better to use newspapers for wrapping than for reading." He placed the newspaper on his giant pile. "Always a bad story. Always something very sad."

She wanted to ask about the cinnamon-smelling boy—was he their son, or nephew, and where was he now? But she couldn't do it.

Finally, on the day she'd decided her browsing was getting ridiculous and she'd better stop hanging out in the shop or they'd put a detective on *her,* he appeared again, just where he had stood the first time, eating yogurt out of a cup.

"What's up?" he said to her, tipping his head and smiling.

"I was taking a walk." She coughed and grew courageous. "I was looking for you."

He raised an interested eyebrow. "Yes?"

"I think we might—have more things to talk about."

Liyana, she said to herself, *Poppy would flip!*

Here, in the land of dignity.

Here, where a girl was hardly supposed to THINK about a boy!

But he didn't flinch. He grinned even more widely. "I'm *sure,*" he said. But he wasn't making fun of her. "I think you are right." His spoon rattled around in his cup. "Shall we talk about—yogurt?"

She took such a deep, relieved breath it sounded as if she were gulping. "I eat another kind without so much writing on the cup," she said. "It tastes saltier and less creamy."

"I prefer it myself," he said. "This kind is more sweet. But the store was finished with—your kind. Do you like yogurt with fruit?"

"I hate it."

"I hate it, too!"

Mr. Sandrouni looked vaguely amused. "Shall we start a taster's club in here when business gets slow?" he said. "You could eat out of my bowls. Don't they have those things—people tasting cheese and wine together?"

Liyana felt a charge of enthusiasm as if such a dopey conversation were electrifying her.

The boy put out his hand. "Don't you think we should trade names now that we know so much about each other?"

She thought he said his name was "Omar" but he went by "Or."

"Why?"

"It's shorter."

When she told him hers, he smiled. "A nice name," he said. "I never heard it before." He said it twice. Liyana thought it rolled around on his tongue.

She asked, "Is your last name Sandrouni?" and he looked startled.

"Me? No way! I'm not related to these guys! I'm just—an old friend of their family!"

Mr. Sandrouni said, "He asked me to adopt him, but I refused."

Liyana and Or made a plan to meet for yogurt at Abu Musa's the next day, after discovering they had exactly the same lunch break.

———

At dinner that night, Liyana did not tell her parents about her new friend. But she asked Poppy, "Have we ever had anyone in our family named Omar?" and he looked puzzled.

"Well, I think way back when your grandfather was young and he used to ride his Arabian horse from the village all the way up to Galilee just to eat the tiny crispy fish that were caught in the sea— then I think we might have had an Omar. Why?"

"Did you know him?"

"No. Maybe I heard a story about him. It's a common name, you know."

Later, as they ate rice pudding, Poppy added, "I met the famous actor, Omar Sharif, in a tiny café in Egypt once. Did I ever tell you that? We shared a table because there weren't many tables. He asked me what I did and I said I was getting ready to go to medical school. Then I asked, 'What about you?'"

"I'm an actor," Omar Sharif said. "I'm getting ready to be a famous actor."

Liyana opened her eyes wider. "Wow, he *knew that? Before it happened?*"

Poppy said, "I had never heard of him. So I answered cockily, if you can believe it—*Isn't everybody an actor?*"

———

At Abu Musa's café, neither Liyana nor Or ordered yogurt. They ordered *hummus,* which came swirled with sprigs of parsley for garnish. They sat at a crooked table outside, dipping their breads into the same creamy plate.

"Did you always live here in Jerusalem?" Liyana asked him and he said, "Always—forever and ever— from the time of the—infinite sorrows—till now."

She liked how he talked. His English was very flowing.

"Do you hope to live in Jerusalem forever?"

She felt like an interviewer. Tiny gray birds poked around their feet for crumbs and pecked at a paper wrapper. Did it taste of salt, of pomegranate syrup, of sesame? Did they fly around the city together or had they met just now for the first time? Liyana tossed them a stalk of parsley.

"Where else would somebody go, after here? Omaha?"

For some reason that struck her funny. Not that she had ever been to Omaha, but just the fact he would think of the *word*.

"I'm sure there are lots of immigrants who have gone to Omaha," she told him.

"But a place is inside you—like a part of your body, don't you think? Like a liver or kidney? So how could you leave it? It sounds like big trouble to me."

She stared at the table. The patterned grains of wood in the scarred surface reminded her of currents in the Mississippi River. Would she ever smell that muggy air again?

"But what do *you* think?" he continued. "Didn't you come here from another place? Do you think I'm wrong?"

A sparrow landed right on her foot and jumped off again. "I'm from St. Louis," she said softly. "Just—a city. Like—Omaha. I don't think you're wrong. But—do you think you can get your kidney back?"

He tapped his finger on the tabletop. He stared at her in a soft way that made her feel warm. Then he said, "I hope so."

Old men were trudging up the skinny street with baskets of kindling tied to their backs. Liyana took a big sip of her lemonade. She felt saddened by their conversation but glad to be mentioning it, at least.

"What do you *do* all the time?" Liyana said. "Where do you go when you're not in school?"

He looked around. She liked the straight line of his jaw, his skin's rich olive tint. "Well, I walk. I walk a lot. I go to the Sandrounis', and the museums, and the libraries, and the soccer fields, and the beach sometimes in summers—do you go to the beach?—and the green country around Nazareth, where my mother is from—have you been there?"

They ordered a bowl of *baba ghanouj* because they were still hungry.

He said tentatively, "I'm also very happy to stay at my house and read books and listen to music."

He had careful fingers. He tore his bread into neat triangles, not ripped hunks, as Rafik did. He offered her more before he took any himself. Liyana realized she was staring at the subtle valley above his upper lip, the small elegant dip under his nose. Did everybody have one of those?

She was staring at his wrist, the graceful way it came out of his sleeve.

"Have you heard any of the new folk music over here?" he asked.

"No," she said. "But I would like to."

He invited her to meet him on Saturday at 1 P.M. at a coffeehouse called "The Fountain" where they had live local music on weekends. "They have orange juice, too—if you don't drink coffee."

She wished she had a pocket calendar. She'd fill in every day.

When they parted to return to their own schools, he took her hand formally and shook it. "Liyana, it was a real pleasure talking with you. Better than most days of my life! And I look forward to our next visit."

"Or," she said, hesitating a moment, because it felt like calling somebody "And" or "But." "Or— I enjoyed it—too."

He gripped her hand a moment extra.

———✦———

Sometimes to hold a good secret inside you made the rest of a day feel glittery. You could move through dull moments without any pain.

All afternoon at her desk, Liyana felt lifted up by the glint of her secret. An invisible humming engine shone a small spotlight onto one corner of her desk, to the upper right of the geometry text, and the triangles they were studying all looked like bread.

$\mathcal{T}$HE FOUNTAIN

If you could be anyone,
would you choose to be yourself?

The day after Thanksgiving, which no one else in
Jerusalem even mentioned, much less celebrated,
Liyana's family sat on the low couches in the living room after dinner reading different sections of
newspaper when she blurted out her plan.

"Fountain? Fountain? Never heard of it," said
Poppy.

"You've never taken the bus alone into the
city," said her mother, putting down her page.

"Well, it can't be very hard," Liyana answered
testily. "I mean, I've taken it coming home, right?
Is there a huge difference? On our road it only
goes north to Ramallah and south to Jerusalem.
I'll take the south one. Then, when I see the city,
which I *do* recognize by now, I'll get off. Then I'll
walk."

"Walk?" they said in unison.

———————

Every day Liyana's father drove her into

Jerusalem, letting her off by Jaffa Gate so she could walk into the Armenian Quarter by herself and go to school. At lunch she hiked miles within the walled city, around curls and corners of tiny alleyways, up secretive staircases, along crowded thoroughfares smelling of oranges and rose water and damp, mopped stone. And now they acted as if she'd never walked before.

"How did you hear of this place? Do your friends at school go there?"

"Well—they *might* if they know about it."

Actually she hadn't mentioned it to any of them. She was still keeping it a secret rolled up tightly inside her.

"Was it in the newspaper?"

"Maybe." So she spread the back pages from both newspapers on the floor and started scouring them. All she found were ads for purchasing a "beautifully sculpted charm replica of the Second Holy Temple in Jerusalem" and a concert by the Jerusalem Woodwind Quintet (the Jewish paper) and giant obituaries and restaurant ads (the Arabic paper).

She stomped into her room and fell down backward on her bed.

A little later, Liyana's mom stepped into the

doorway of her room and smiled the motherly smile that says, *"I know where you are and I remember being there myself."*

Her mother said, "You know, I have a few errands in the city myself. Would that make things easier? If I drove you and dropped you off and came back to get you?"

"What are your errands?"

"Well, I need to go to a tailor, for one. The two denim skirts I bought right before we left the States are a little too big. I should have tried them on."

"That will take about ten seconds."

"And I'd like to find the vitamin store I heard about. We're running out of Cs and Es. And I need to explore more of the Jewish neighborhoods on foot because I want to find out what's—available. You know how Poppy only takes us around east Jerusalem because he doesn't *know* the other side? Well, I'm ready to discover it. All that might give you two hours or more."

———

Saturday arrived and Liyana rebraided her hair ten times. Then she brushed it and decided to leave it loose. It had little waves in it from all the activity. Her mother, who was not yet used to driving in the city, still pumped the gas hesitantly and everyone passed them. Even very old men passed them.

Liyana said, "Mom, I'm meeting a friend there."

"From school?"

"Not my school."

"A girl?"

"Not a girl."

Her mother's foot hit the brake a little. "You mean—this is—a date?"

"Not a date. It's an—appointment."

"Who is he?"

"He's Or."

"What?"

"For Omar. I met him—at the Sandrounis' ceramics shop. The place Poppy showed me. I was—just in there—a few times."

"He works there?"

"No. They're friends."

Liyana could see right then she had rounded the bend where conversations with her parents were no longer going to be as easy as they once were.

"Do you know what your father would say?"

"About what?"

"Liyana! This is his country. It is a very conservative country. Haven't you noticed? Remember the shorts? Remember his story about someone getting in trouble in the village simply because he talked to a woman in the street? People have supposedly even been killed! For little indiscretions! I realize you are not a villager and you don't have to live by their old-fashioned codes. Just remember your father won't like it if he knows about it. Still, I think you should tell him. Absolutely. Tonight at dinnertime. Or the minute we get home. And— oh Liyana, be careful. Be—*appropriate*."

There it was. The word she hated most.

⸺

They parked on a side street near the Old City. Or had described to her how to walk to The Fountain.

"Where's the tailor?" Liyana asked Mom, who was carrying her skirts bunched up in one arm, and her mother said, "Who knows? I'm looking for her."

Liyana struggled to remember Or's directions exactly—up one hill, past the odd windmill, to the right, then straight. The streets seemed wider on this side of town. They passed a store for watches, a bank, a gift shop full of antiques, a nursery school. Fewer sounds of Arabic drifted through the air now—just the husky, less familiar-sounding accents of Hebrew and languages they couldn't identify. Norwegian, Liyana thought. Polish or Russian.

She recognized The Fountain by the courtyard in front of it containing chairs, striped umbrella tables, and—yes—a fountain spurting water from two crossed jugs into a blue pool.

Someone in the cheery interior adjusted a microphone on a stage. A lady with a deep tan, bright lipstick, and a pink drink at an outdoor table turned her cheek up to the sun. Liyana didn't see Or anywhere.

"Are you sure this is it?"

"Yes." Two dark birds dipped into the fountain and splashed themselves.

Liyana didn't know how to make it sound sweeter, so she just blurted it out. "Could you please go on now?"

Her mother looked slightly hurt but not terribly.

They decided to meet by the windmill in two hours since there was only one and it was easy to find.

Just before Liyana stepped inside the café by herself, Or materialized beside her. "You made it! You remembered my directions!"

She could have told him she remembered even the smallest brown hairs on the back of his hand.

"There is bad news," he said. "The person I hoped was playing and singing is not here today. Another person is playing who, I am sorry to say..." he whispered into her ear, "is very terrible."

"Would you like to go to the Israel Museum instead?" he asked straight into her ear. "It's not far away." She had never been there. Poppy had talked about going one day, but they got side-tracked into visiting the tomb of Lazarus instead.

"Uh—sure." But she felt a little worried. Her mother and father never liked it when she and Rafik changed their plans without telling them.

The Israel Museum, largest in the country, displayed archaeological wonders and contemporary art. Liyana had been reading about its shows and lectures in the newspaper. One Saturday, sleepily thumbing through the newspaper at the breakfast table, she'd suggested to Rafik that he attend a youth workshop on "developing artistic talents."

He said he had all the talents he could handle right now.

Later he asked her, "Am I the only youth in this house?"

Liyana followed Or up the street. He waved at shopkeepers and said something to an old woman passing in a black dress and black scarf.

Then it struck her. He said it in Hebrew!

A yellow cat dodged a black car. Her heart was pounding. Two young women in blue jeans walked by chattering, pushing baby buggies.

She didn't know how to ask him this.

"Or," she stuttered, "did you—are you—what did you—say to her?"

"Her husband died a few months ago," he answered. "She's a neighbor of ours. We took food to her house during the first week of mourning, when she and her family were sitting *shiva*—that time when the family doesn't wear shoes or leave the house, when they cover all their mirrors. This is the first day I've seen her out in the world again. "

"Cover all the mirrors," Liyana repeated. "That's a—powerful tradition. It's a—Jewish tradition?"

He looked at her curiously. "Yes, it's a Jewish tradition. And I think you may have some similar Arabic traditions, too."

As her heart jogged and blipped, she said, "Well, they won't listen to music in the village, after someone dies. I don't know about the mirrors. Come to think of it, I don't know if they *have* any mirrors."

Liyana's mind flew forward at full speed. She realized there shouldn't be anything shocking about his being Jewish in a place made up mostly of Arabs and Jews. It's just that she hadn't even *thought* of it. And wasn't his name "Omar" an Arabic name?

When she mentioned this, stuttering, he laughed roundly so his fabulous teeth showed. "*Omer,* my friend," he said, "with an *e* not an *a*— which is a Jewish name. You don't like it as much?"

She thought, *It's stupid for my heart to race.*

"Could we sit down a minute?" she asked. They sat on a wall beside a cedar tree and she took a deep breath.

"Did you know I wasn't Jewish?" she asked him.

"Of course."

"How?"

"Well, you were carrying Arabic copybooks in your satchel, for one thing. Those little gray notebooks for homework? And you told me you live on the Ramallah road, didn't you? I don't have any *other* friends who live on the Ramallah road."

"Does that bother you?" she asked.

"Ha! Would I suggest we get together—if it bothered me? The question is—does it bother *you?*"

"Of course not," she said, startled, as words came out of her mouth that she could not predict from minute to minute. "I'm an American," she said. "Mostly." But that sounded ridiculous. He hadn't asked for her passport. "I mean, this fighting is senseless, don't you think? People should be able to get over their differences by this time, but they just stay mad. They have their old reasons or they find new ones. I mean, I understand it mostly from the Arab side because my father's family lost their house and their money in the bank and lots of their community when my father was a boy and the Palestinians were suffering so much, just kicked around till recently as if they were second-class human beings you know they couldn't even show their own flag or have hardly any normal human rights like the Jews did till recently and it's getting better only slowly you know my relatives have to get permits for things all the time and it wasn't that way when my father was little, things were more equal then and of course I know the Jewish people suffered so much themselves, but don't you think it should have made them more sensitive to the sufferings of others, too?"

Her mouth had become a fountain. Spurting waterfalls of words.

He stared at her quietly. "I do."

Birds jabbered in branches above them. Flit and bustle. What did people seem like to birds?

Omer took a deep breath and stood up. "It's a bad history without a doubt," he said. "Nothing to be proud of." He closed his eyes, turning his face to the side, right into the sun. "So what are we going to do about it?" Then he opened his eyes, made a little bow, and put his hand out toward the avenue, as if to offer her the street.

Liyana thought, *Now he'll hate me. I'm a talking maniac.* As a kind of finishing touch, Liyana blurted, "I have hope for the peace, do you?" And he stared at her closely. "Of course I do. Would you still like to go to the museum?"

———

They walked up the street without speaking, their arms brushing a few times. Liyana thought, *My mother's probably watching us from the window of the bank across the street, her mouth wide open with shock that I'm not where I said I would be.*

———

Inside the massive museum, Liyana and Omer stared happily at giant paintings, sculptures, and ancient lamps dug out of caves. They made themselves pay polite attention to the older art, though they both agreed they were more interested in the odd contemporary rooms.

Liyana liked how Omer stood back from pieces, then moved in to examine them closely, and drifted back again. She still felt breathless from her outburst. He seemed calmly deliberate, paying close attention. He shook his head over a painting that was nothing but bright red slashes, quick thick lines. He said, "My eyes don't like it. Do yours?" Liyana wondered why it was such a relief to dislike the same things your friends did. What did that tell you about a person?

"Do you mind," she asked, "if I call you by your whole name instead of your nickname?"

He said, "I don't mind if you give me a new name I never heard before."

Omer was wearing a thick, white, long-sleeved T-shirt with three buttons at the throat, blue jeans, and purple high-topped tennis shoes. She liked his clothes. She could easily have stared at him more than the artwork, but tried to keep her gaze on the walls whenever she was in his vision. Her eyes rose into a turquoise horizon. She floated on the ripe blue cloud an artist had painted crowning a yellow city. Was that Jerusalem? Sometimes Omer stood behind her and she heard his breathing as they viewed the same piece. She felt a delicious jitter inside.

One artist offered a giant bright installation titled "Underground Springs" made from tin cans roped together, painted flashing purple and silver, spilling forth from a map of Israel on the wall. Omer laughed out loud. "Do you worry about it?" he asked. "Where all the trash will be ten years from now? I worry about it every time I open a can of tuna fish."

"Tuna fish?" Liyana said. It was one of the things her mother had been looking for in their Arab stores, but Arabs didn't like tuna much. "Can you get it over here?"

"Of course. It's delicious with yogurt." He poked her in the side. Other foods the Abbouds missed crowded her mind. Should she ask? Lima beans! Lemon meringue pie!

When she finally remembered to glance at her watch, she exclaimed so loudly, a dozing guard over in the corner jumped. "Oh my! I forgot to meet my mother! I'm ten minutes late already!"

She and Omer sprinted toward the windmill, where they found her mother tapping her foot and staring at her watch, arms crammed with packages. When she saw them (about twenty-five minutes late by now) she said to Liyana, "I thought maybe you'd gone onto daylight savings time."

"Mom, I'm so sorry! The time—slipped away from us. We ended up going to the museum instead, I hope that's okay with you, you would have loved it!—you know that big one I've been wanting to go to? Anyway, this is Omer, my friend I mentioned."

Her mother greeted Omer with interest, but couldn't shake his hand since hers were loaded. Omer reached out and insisted on carrying almost all her bags to their car. Liyana could see she was impressed by his manners.

"I found it!" her mother said over her shoulder to Liyana. "Mayonnaise!" Omer raised his eyebrows. Liyana felt trembly and weak. She hoped her mother wouldn't say other goofy family stuff. But her mother smoothly turned her attention to Omer, smiling that generic mother smile.

"Have you always lived in Jerusalem? Do you like your school? Are you familiar with Liyana's school? Do you know other people who go there? What do you most like to do in your spare time?"

He said, "Wander. Both inside and outside my head." Her mother looked at Liyana as if she could now see how the two of them were connected.

In the car on the way home, her mother said calmly, "Liyana, I don't think he is an Arab."

Liyana said, "So?" which was not the way to answer your mother when you wanted to keep her on your side. But that's what came out.

They drove in silence for a mile, past the Universal Laundry and Abdul Rahman's shoe repair shop where Liyana's favorite beat-up American loafers were currently taking a vacation, awaiting new soles. Liyana said, "No one I go to school with is an Arab either. Did you know they made me an honorary Armenian citizen?"

Her mother looked sideways at her. "You know what I mean."

Liyana swallowed twice. "We already talked about it. He believes in the peace as much as we do."

A crowd of old women with baskets on their

arms waited for a bus. Her mother paused a long time before saying, "I just fear your father's response. Of all the boys you might find in this town to have a crush on…"

Liyana kept plummeting. "Can he come over? For dinner someday soon? He gave me his telephone number and I gave him ours!"

"Don't you start calling him, Missy," her mother said, and Liyana opened and closed her mouth like a fish. If she didn't, she might suffocate.

<hr />

At dinner, Poppy said starkly, "What? Who? Where?"

Liyana said, "This isn't a book report, you know." Then she said, "Remember when you told us how you had Jewish neighbors and friends when you were growing up here? Remember how we had plenty of Jewish friends back in the United States? Why not? He lives on Rashba Street. Did you ever go to Rashba Street when you were little?"

Poppy said, "Sure." But a moment later he said, "Never, never, never."

<hr />

All evening Liyana stood by her window staring west toward Jewish Israel. She had a new feeling about it. The guard at the museum quietly locked the galleries. The paintings slept calmly on their walls. Over there the Mediterranean's soft blue waves were scattering shells. Liyana had never yet been to a beach in this country. She thought she'd like to visit one with Omer. They could take their shoes and watches off and walk and walk for miles. They could sink their feet into the sand.

WE WISH YOU A MERRY EVERYTHING

Would a wise man please step forward?

At Christmas time, Jerusalem and Bethlehem felt crisp and cool, flickering with candles in windows, buttery yellow streetlights, and music floating from shops—thin threads of light and sound. But the holiday decorations weren't nearly as prominent or glossy as they were in American cities. "I don't think Santa Claus made it over here yet," mourned Rafik.

"Sometimes," Liyana mused, "when you're standing in the places where important things really happened, it's even harder to imagine them. Don't you think? Because video stores and Christmas pilgrims unfolding Walking Tour maps are getting in your way. History is hiding."

"Thank you," said Rafik. "Thank you for your wisdoms."

At midnight on Christmas Eve they stood with their parents in the long line at the Church of the Nativity in Bethlehem. Poppy had done this as a teenager himself, with his Arab Christian friends. Liyana and Rafik both had checkered black and white *kaffiyehs* wrapped around their necks against the chill. Irish nuns harmonized in wavery soprano voices. Liyana and her mother led a few verses of "Angels We Have Heard On High." A gold star on the floor inside marked the spot where the manger might have been. It was the one "official" spot that didn't make Mom feel like crying.

Liyana liked to remind herself: *Jesus had a real body. Jesus had baby's breath.*

And Jesus did not write the list of rules posted on the stone wall. There were many, but Liyana's eyes caught on the first: No ARMS ALLOWED INSIDE THIS CHURCH.

$\mathscr{A}$ KERNEL OF TRUTH ON EVERY AVENUE

She really believed her parents
when they said, "Look both ways."

On one of the first warm days, Omer and Liyana licked pistachio ice cream cones as they sat on an iron bench near the Russian Orthodox Church with its onion domes. They were waiting for Hagop and Atom from Liyana's class to appear so they could go see a French movie at the British library.

Omer asked, "What religion are you?"

The Abbouds had never belonged to a church since Liyana was born, but it might have made things easier. Liyana's mother said they were a *spiritual* family, they just weren't a *traditionally religious* one.

Most people said, "Huh?"

They wanted you to say, "I'm this kind of letter and I go in this kind of envelope."

Omer knew exactly what she was talking about the minute she started to describe it. He said people always asked *him* if he was religious or secular. He would say, "I have Jewish hands,

Jewish bones, Jewish stories, and a Jewish soul. But I'm not officially observant of—the religious practices of the Jewish people. Got it?" His family did a few special-holiday things.

Liyana's family believed in God and goodness and hope and positive thinking and praying. They believed in the Golden Rule—*Do unto others as you would have them do unto you*—who didn't? A mosquito didn't.

Liyana's mother believed a *whole* lot in karma, the Hindu belief that what someone does in this world will come back to him or her—maybe not the day after tomorrow, but eventually. Liyana also liked the eightfold path in Buddhism, and the idea of the *bodhisattva,* the soul who does good for others without any thought for himself or herself. She hoped she would get to know some in her life, besides her parents. Rafik believed in sandalwood incense.

Liyana's entire family believed in reincarnation because it made sense to them. They didn't want to have to say good-bye for good so soon. Poppy said he'd like a thousand lives. Rafik wanted to be reborn in Japan so he could ride the bullet train.

"But what about all these *new* people?" Omer asked her. "Where did *they* come from? You know, the population explosion?"

"I don't know. Maybe souls can split or something." Liyana wasn't too interested in the details.

She just liked thinking of different lives as chain links, connected. She had always felt homesick for some other life, even when she was a baby standing in her crib wearing a diaper not knowing any words yet.

Liyana's parents did not believe everyone was an automatic sinner when they were born. Too dramatic! All people on earth would do good and bad things both. Poppy said every religion contained some shining ideas and plenty of foolishness, too.

"The worst foolish thing is when a religion wants you to say it's the only right one. Or the best one. That's when I pack my bags and start rolling."

He was always rolling, Poppy Abboud. Out of one good story into another one. He didn't like fancy church buildings either. "What *else* could they have done with their money? They could have helped the poor people, for one thing!"

Once in the United States some ladies came knocking at the Abbouds' door when Poppy was home alone. "We'd like to tell you about Jesus Christ," they announced, and he thought to himself, "I was born in Jerusalem, right down the road from Bethlehem, and they think they're just now telling me?"

But he said, "Come in, come in." Excusing

himself for a moment, he marched into his bedroom, tied on a long gray cloak that had belonged to his father, and a checkered *kaffiyeh,* the headdress that he never really wore, and leapt out of the bedroom into their startled gaze.

"But *first,*" he said, "may I tell you about Muhammad?"

They left the house that instant and never returned.

———

The Abbouds did not believe in the devil, except the devilish spirit inside people doing bad things. They did not believe in hell, or anybody being "chosen" over anybody else—which Liyana had to ask Omer about. He looked sober. He told her the Jewish idea of being "chosen" meant more than he could explain. "Maybe Jews are also chosen to suffer. Or to be better examples."

Liyana said, "It seems like big trouble any way you look at it. I'm sorry, but I don't like it. Do you *believe* you're chosen? It sounds like the teacher's pet."

He didn't know what that was. "It's not a question of *believing,*" he said.

"What do you mean?"

Omer said, "It's more like—history. A historical way of—looking at ourselves—and things."

Liyana felt gloomy. "And it's history that gave us all these problems," she said. "I think as long as anybody feels *chosen,* the problems will get worse."

Omer asked, "But what about your father's family in the village? Don't they try to make you become Muslim like they are?"

"No. Not yet, anyway."

Omer said, "I'd like to meet them. Do you think I could—go with you someday?"

"I hope so!" Liyana said.

———

Poppy knew from when he was a boy there must be a *kernel of truth on every avenue.* He *thought* about the reasons behind different beliefs—no pork, for example, came from the old days when pork was the first meat to spoil. "Does it make sense," Poppy said, "that any God would choose some people and leave the others out? If only Christians or Jews are right, what about most of Asia and the Middle East? All these millions of people are just—extras? Ridiculous! God's bigger than that!"

Any kind of fundamentalism gave Poppy the shivers. The Jews in Hebron called themselves "holy pioneers." "Fundamentalists talk louder than liberals," he said. "That's too bad. Maybe we moderate people should raise our voices."

When Liyana told this to Omer, he said, "Your father's right. Please, I want to meet him!"

———

On the other side of the earth, Peachy Helen's parents had believed their Christian denomination was "chosen" too. They were the only ones going to be "saved"—but Peachy refused to raise her own children that way.

Peachy Helen had often taken Liyana's mother to the art museum instead of to church. They would stare into blue and green paintings by Monet. "Look at the wavery edges of things! *That's* how we could live."

When Liyana's mother had measles as a girl, she lay in bed for a week in a dim room with lowered shades. She lay as still as a cucumber on a vine.

"Peachy Helen stood over me saying prayers of healing that she made up as she went along. She said, I hope they'll work if they're not official. First she cried, then we both laughed together. I promised her I would get well. And of course I did. But it was then I realized I had been grumpy sometimes for no reason. After that, I thought of every day as A FRESH CHOICE!" She talked about it in capital letters as if it were a feature at the grocery store. "My mother sang a song to keep me calm, "Look for the Silver Lining." The same one I taught to you."

Mrs. Abboud had told Rafik and Liyana to carry the song as a crucial part of their memory banks. Liyana had a stomachache when they learned it so she kept picturing the inside of her stomach coated with silver. They made Peachy Helen pay a nickel to hear them sing it. Sometimes Liyana thought of that song as their religion.

When Liyana and Rafik were little, their mother took them to the art museum *and* to a rich assortment of Sunday schools—Methodist, Presbyterian, Episcopalian, Unity, and Unitarian—where they signed in as "visitors," wore the yellow visitor ribbons, and sometimes kept coming back for months. They just didn't *join* anything. Poppy stayed home reading the newspaper or digging in the garden.

"Didn't the churches wonder where you went when you disappeared?" Omer asked.

"I guess we seemed like hoboes."

"What's a hobo?"

Then they talked about wanderers and gypsies and vagabonds longer than they talked about anything else.

———

Liyana's parents would discuss religion late into the

night in the living room when Liyana was in bed. She would listen to them till their words blended into a soft sheet of sleep gently spreading over her.

Their words made sense. Why *would* any God want to be only large enough to fit inside a certain group of hearts? God was a Big God. Once Liyana answered someone that way, but it didn't work very well.

"What religion are you?"

"Big God."

It sounded like the Big Sam Shop, where truck drivers bought new tires.

—————

Some people let their countries become their religions and that didn't work either. Liyana thought it would never happen to her. She never even felt like a Full and Total American, except maybe when her kindergarten class said the Pledge of Allegiance with hands on their hearts and she was proud to know the fat fruits of words between her lips— republic, nation, indivisible—what a pleasure just to say *words* that felt bigger than you were.

Liyana knew *indivisible* even when her friends still thought it was *invisible,* but she didn't tell them because there are things you have to find out for yourself.

*W*ATER AND ASHES

> *When we were born*
> *we were blank pieces of paper;*
> *nothing had been written yet.*

On Rafik and Liyana's birthdays, Poppy always brought flowers to their mother. He wanted to thank her for having had such wonderful kids. The day before Liyana's fifteenth birthday, he stepped through the door after work with a hefty bouquet of white roses, saying, "What do you think? Fifteen deserves something—regal!"

Their mother was still at the English radio station where she worked three days a week now. Rafik liked to say, "Our mother is a DJ," but the station was mostly news, interviews, and cooking programs. Liyana dug under the sink for a glass jar to put the roses in.

The phone rang and Rafik answered it. He called to his dad, "Quick! I know it's Sitti, but I don't know what she's saying! She's shouting loud! I think she's crying too." Liyana froze.

Poppy let the roses dangle upside down as he

listened. Liyana rescued them, her blood buzzing. Usually Abu Daoud conveyed Sitti's messages, or she yelled into the phone from a distance. She didn't like to hold the receiver because she thought it might shock her.

Poppy asked a few questions, then was silent a long time. Finally he slammed down the phone. He'd just told Sitti they'd be there right away. "What, what?" Rafik and Liyana asked him at once.

"I'll tell you in the car."

He was out the door already.

———

Driving too fast to the village, Poppy said Israeli soldiers had appeared at Sitti's house and demanded to see her grandson Mahmud, who'd been living in Jordan for the past two years. He was studying to be a pharmacist. Poppy had told Liyana she would like him because he had a good sense of humor, but she hadn't had a chance to meet him yet.

Sitti told the soldiers, "He's not home," because that was the way she talked about him— as if he might turn the corner any moment. "He's not home, but he might be coming soon." She could have said that about anybody, even her dead husband, the way she thought of things.

Poppy said the soldiers pushed past her into the house and searched it, dumping out drawers, ripping comforters from the cupboards. Sitti said, "He's not in *there*." They broke the little blue plate she loved. "What are you doing?" she screamed. There were four of them.

Then they went into Sitti's bathroom and smashed the bathtub with hard metal clubs they were carrying.

Rafik said, "Smashed the bathtub? Why?" Liyana felt nervous wondering, were those soldiers still around? What if they got into a—tango— with them?

Poppy said, "They smashed the sink so it cracked into big pieces on the floor and water streamed from the broken faucets into the room and Sitti was terrified. She thought she was going to drown. She thought water would fill up the whole house, but of course it must have poured into the courtyard and Abu Daoud heard her screams from next door and came running over. He turned off the water at the pipe, I think. Anyway, she said it's not gushing now. Then the soldiers smashed the toilet—"

Rafik interrupted. "WHY?"

Poppy swerved to avoid a sheep in the road. His voice sounded tight and hard. "THERE IS NO WHY. I am filling up to my throat from these stories. Do you know how many of them I hear every day from my patients at work? I don't tell you. I can't tell you. And I thought things were getting better over here."

Liyana said quietly, "I thought there was always a why."

Shadows stretched across the road, late afternoon, a softness falling down from the sky no matter what people did.

———

At Sitti's house, a small crowd of men and women had gathered tensely outside. They nodded at Poppy and his children as they passed. Rafik entered first and shouted, "Sitti's house is a mess!"

Sitti was mopping and crying all at once. Liyana tried to take the mop from her hand and she brushed her away. An old lady Liyana didn't recognize was down on her knees scrubbing the floor with pieces of rags.

Everyone kept muttering about the soldiers. Poppy translated. *The soldiers left in a truck. We hate their truck. We thought they weren't supposed to bother us anymore. We thought the peace said they would stay away.*

What did they want? They wanted Mahmud. WHY? For two hours Poppy talked to everybody. Nobody knew. Mahmud read books. Books could be dangerous? Poppy tried to phone the police in Ramallah, but the phone line was blank. The soldiers had cut it. Poppy put his hands to his head. He shook his head, saying, "They must do it because it's personal. It's insulting. And it's weird."

He tried to calm Sitti down, but she was inconsolable, whimpering like a cat. Liyana thought she was sadder about the blue plate than the toilet. Sitti kept fingering its pieces, trying to fit them together.

Rafik and Liyana sat in the corner, invisible as the lemons in the bowl on the second shelf. Bathrooms were not cheap. Sitti was not rich.

She reluctantly agreed to spend the night at Aunt Saba's house, folding a dress to wear the next day and her prayer rug and a towel. She mumbled something under her breath.

They walked with her through a stunned village. Even the scrappy birds seemed quieter. Even the children who usually called out from rooftops weren't making any sound.

~

In Ramallah, Poppy stopped at a store open late for plumbing parts, so he could engage a plumber to head to Sitti's house the next day. At home, their mother was frantic. She met them at the top of the steps. "No note? Do you realize what *time* it is?"

After Rafik told what had happened, she was silent. Then she shouted, "NO! That poor little bathroom! But why? Why the bathroom?"

Liyana quoted, "There is no why." It was strange how quickly someone else's words could come out of your mouth. Idly lifting the front section of the newspaper, she read that a Jewish deputy mayor of Jerusalem proposed two thousand Arab homes in east Jerusalem be torn down to make room for fifty thousand houses for Jews. It didn't say anything about pain or attachment or sorrow or honor.

Liyana slipped outside with the front page and the box of kitchen matches.

On a bare patch of earth, Liyana lit two edges of newspaper. They caught slowly at first, then burst into a cone of bright flame. The fire ate the words. Fire ate them inside and out. Liyana blew the ashes into the dust.

Later Sitti would tell them her new bathtub swallowed water with the sound of a cow.

FIFTEEN

Before anything was written, where was I?

That night Liyana dreamed a cake fell off its plate into the sea and floated away from her. She reached wildly with both her arms, standing knee-deep in the pull of powerful waves.

And it was Omer she was calling to. "Save it! Can you reach it?" but he was swimming too far out. Then she was shouting and waving, "I'm sorry! I wanted to share it with you!" but he could not hear her. He was swimming the other direction. And the cake was drowning.

When Liyana woke on her birthday, her mother was singing in the hallway. Poppy joined in off-key as he stepped into the bathroom and Rafik pretended to be playing a trombone. "Pancakes for breakfast!"

Liyana's place at the breakfast table was surrounded by cheerful hand-drawn cards with yellow Magic Marker daisies. "A decade and a half!" Rafik had written. "Is that an antique yet?"

Poppy wrote half his card in English and half in Arabic. "To my soon-to-be-bilingual daughter," the English said. Liyana could make out letters in Arabic by now—ones that looked like chimneys or fluted edges, but she couldn't really make out *words* yet. So he helped her read it. *"I'm proud of you. What a year it's been!"*

Mom's just said, "To my queen—at 15" in calligraphy. She was already stirring up batter for a pineapple upside-down cake, Liyana's favorite. "I had a weird dream about a cake," Liyana said.

When Poppy went downstairs to get his gift for Liyana out of the trunk of the car (fifteen new notebooks, including some fancy European ones, and fifteen new pens), he found a mysterious silver package sitting on the step. He carried it upstairs held far out from his body, saying, "Isn't it sad what one thinks about these days? Should we get a bomb-sniffing dog? In the old days people never thought about such things."

Since it had Liyana's name handwritten and spelled correctly on a card at the top, she opened it and gasped.

Inside was the green lamp she'd first asked Omer about, at the Sandrounis' ceramics shop, the one too expensive to buy for herself.

A tightly folded note was taped to it. "Don't worry, I traded labor, not cash. Happy birthday! Omer."

Liyana wondered how he got to her house so

early to deliver it. He must have taken a taxi from Jerusalem, dropped it off, and ridden the same taxi back.

Poppy said dourly, "Is this an appropriate gift for a young man to give a young woman?"

Her mother said, "It's fine! It's not jewelry or clothing. It's not silver or gold. Don't give her any trouble!"

———

All day at school, when Liyana described the scene of Sitti's bathroom smashing, the chips of ceramic and waterlogged rooms, her classmates shrugged. People got used to disasters. No one was even killed.

Liyana felt distracted during class. She always had mixed feelings on her birthdays. She gazed out the school window at the changing clouds, casting a flurry of words toward Omer's side of the city. *I miss you. I want to see you. You would never do something like those soldiers did.* But she wrote only five words down in her new notebook: *I love your amazing memory.*

HISTORY OF KISSING

*I would like to know
the story of every little thing.*

Rafik and Liyana dressed one of the sleeping chickens in the henhouse in a brocade tunic Liyana had sewn especially for her, from a wide silver and burgundy scrap her friend Bilal had given her. They imagined what it would be like for Imm Janan, their landlord's sleepy wife, to discover her hen wearing a lavish robe, as if she'd been crowned queen at midnight.

Liyana had had a hard time sewing the thing so the hen's legs could poke out where they needed to. She even "fitted her" once, in the dark. Rafik wanted Liyana to sew a bonnet as well, but she thought that might be a little much.

The hen mumbled cozily in their hands. Liyana said, "I hope this won't give her bad dreams or anything." Once the robe was tied on and the hen's legs came through the bottom, she rippled her body back and forth, as if to see how much she could still move. Did she think it was a new suit of feathers?

They photographed her with their mother's flash camera, which seemed to upset her more than the dress did.

Rafik said, "I don't think she likes having her wings pressed down." But she settled back into her nest and closed her eyes.

The next morning they were anxious to get to the American Library, where they often went on Saturdays to do their hideous homework. Afterward they'd meet Poppy for lunch and have minty ice cream at the YMCA next door. At breakfast, Rafik kept glancing out the window toward the henhouse. He said, "Drive us, Poppy, let's go now!" What if Imm Janan saw the chicken and screamed instead of laughed? They wanted to be gone when she discovered it.

———

At their gleaming library table, Liyana felt distracted. She kept getting up to pull reference books off the shelves and flip through their pages. She found some really old ones about Palestine with intricate drawings of the Old City in them. In a 1926 book called *Life in Palestine When Jesus Lived,* she read, "...the people were constantly at work... How many languages were spoken, what differences of color, look, habit, manner, dress, must have been seen!"

On her birthday after school, she had called Omer to thank him for the wonderful surprise, and his mother, who didn't speak English very well, answered the phone. Liyana had to ask for him three times.

Omer seemed shy when she raved over her lamp. He just said, "Read some good books under it, okay?" and asked what she had been doing lately. They hadn't been able to share their lunch breaks for a few weeks since he'd been practicing for a debate tournament with his team at lunchtime. Liyana had mentioned more than once that she and Rafik would be studying at the American Library in Jerusalem on Saturday. Now she kept hoping secretly Omer would show up.

So when the heavy green library door squeaked open again, after admitting nuns and the Italian man who ran the matches factory and his daughters and six blond tourists with turquoise backpacks, and Omer finally stepped through, wearing a checkered yellow shirt and looking quizzical, Liyana rose joyously to greet him and they hugged tightly for the first time. She pressed her face against his shoulder. It smelled like sun.

Liyana introduced Omer to Rafik, who said only, "Is it true you play soccer?"

Omer folded a small *origami* ball for him from a piece of notebook paper, and batted it across the table. "I made the ball so you make the goal," he whispered.

They tackled their respective heaps of homework, whispering, laughing, and joking till the librarian stood over their table, saying, "You will please keep your silence or I will be forced to ask you to leave." Then it was harder than ever not to laugh.

Liyana was writing about Mark Twain, since he too had lived in Missouri, her old state, and no one else in her class had chosen an American for their author's report. Everyone else was doing someone like Shakespeare, Dante, or John Milton. When she went to search for the library's tattered copy of *Huckleberry Finn* on the far shelves of "Fiction"—to compare the older edition with her own—Omer walked to the end of the same aisle to study the giant Map of the World on the wall, copying some town names from Russia in his notebook. "We have to write about the places our ancestors came from," he said. She had not known his grandparents were from Russia till now.

Liyana kept thinking how everybody was a little like everybody else and nobody was the *same*. She thought of those snowflake and fingerprint stories about the perfect uniqueness of each one and wondered, "Are we supposed to feel good about that?" She *wanted* one snowflake to resemble another one now and then. She even imagined she carried some essence of Mark Twain inside herself, which was why he appealed to her so much. Twain didn't like the Middle East, though. She wouldn't quote anything he'd said on his dopey travels through the Middle East.

Somehow she couldn't bear to return to their table while Omer still stood at the end of the aisle. She felt suspended, reading spines of other books, held fast by his presence close by. She whispered *chillywilly* under her breath. He turned, then, and caught her staring at his back. He came over beside her and whispered, "What are you thinking about?"

Her throat felt thick with a wish to say, simply, "You" but she said, "Mark Twain."

He touched her elbow gently, leaned forward, and placed his beautiful mouth on hers.

A kiss. Wild river. Sudden over stones. As startling as the first time, but nicer, since it happened in the light.

And bigger than the whole deep ache of blue.

It didn't go away right away.

It held, as Omer gently held her elbow cupped in his hand. Warmth spilled between them.

"Liyana," he said. "I—like you."

"Oh!" She said, "Me too. I like *you*."

He said, "You are not—mad?"

"No!"

He smiled, "I don't think the books—are mad." He kissed her again, on her right cheek only, delicately as a feather's touch, and the librarian pushed a cart past their aisle, not even glancing in their direction.

⁂

After they returned in their newly dazzled state to the cluttered table where Rafik was drawing an elaborate soccer field on four pieces of notebook paper laid out end to end, Omer leaned over him and said, "I have bad news, new friend. I have to go to my own soccer game—right now. Would you like to come with me?"

Rafik couldn't, because he and Liyana were meeting Poppy at the Philadelphia for a late lunch at two. But Liyana could tell he was pleased.

Liyana and Omer traded a long gaze as he left. They grinned easily. She placed one finger on her vivid lips. Rafik didn't notice.

Then she walked over to "Reference" and slid an encyclopedia off a shelf to see if "Kissing" had an entry, but nothing appeared between Kishinev, the capital of the Moldavian Soviet Socialist Republic of the USSR, and Kissinger, Henry, born in Germany and a naturalized American like her father. Well, she thought, sort of like her father. Her father didn't care for him. There was no "kissing" in the encyclopedia. She wondered, "Where did kissing come from? Who started it?"

She knew about the Eskimo tribes who liked nose rubbing more than kissing. She was glad she hadn't been born into one. She made a kissing list in her notebook:

> *Lemony lips,*
> *warm magnets pulling toward one*
>   *another,*
> *streets crisscrossed by invisible tugs,*
> *secret power fields.*
> *Electrodynamics.*

Then she wandered over to the "Newly Arrived" shelf (she thought she should live on that shelf herself) and placed her hand directly on a book called *A Natural History of the Senses* by Diane Ackerman. Flipping it open, she discovered a whole astonishing chapter called "Kissing" in the section called "Touch"!

She took the book to their table spread with Rafik's information on famous rivers of the world and shielded it from Rafik to read, *"There are wild, hungry kisses or there are rollicking kisses, and there are kisses fluttery and soft as the feathers of cockatoos."* Liyana had never touched a cockatoo, but she liked how it sounded.

She wrote down a "first line" that said: *Being good felt like a heavy coat, so I took it off.*

The author, Diane, talked about her memory of kissing in high school, using a rich string of adverbs—"inventively...extravagantly...delicately ...elaborately...furtively when we met in the hall-ways between classes...soulfully in the shadows at concerts...we kissed articles of clothing or objects belonging to our boyfriends...we kissed our hands when we blew our boyfriends kisses across the street...we kissed our pillows at night...." OH!

And Liyana knew this book was for her. Because last night, the very night before today, she had kissed her pillow and thought she might be cracking up.

$\mathcal{G}$OAT CHEESE

Drop in anytime and stay forever.

Poppy said their skins would feel so sticky after plunging into the Dead Sea, they'd have to lie down under freshwater spigots to wash off.

He drove Liyana, Rafik, Khaled, and Nadine on the descending road through sand dunes toward Jericho because Rafik had been bugging him so much. Mrs. Abboud had gone on a weekend retreat with her women's group. The women were going to hike ten miles through the wilderness to see some hermit nuns who wouldn't be hermits anymore once they got there.

Liyana and Rafik had bathing suits on under their clothes, bottled water, towels, and a basket of small bananas. Liyana hadn't worn her baggy old-man shorts after all. She'd decided to make them into a purse. Khaled and Nadine said they would go swimming in their clothes. They brought extra clothes rolled up and tied with a string.

Sunlight vibrated on the golden sand. Graceful dunes cast shadows on one another. There weren't any clouds. It felt wonderful to leave the clutter of town behind.

Around a curve, Rafik shouted, "Stop!"

Poppy hated when someone yelled in a car. He braked sharply and pulled over. The roads didn't have shoulders like they did back home. "Don't scare me! What is it?"

Rafik pointed. "I want to visit them."

Poppy and Liyana in the front seat hadn't even noticed the Bedouin tents perched far from the road in a crevice of shade between two dunes. They'd been talking about Sitti's new obsession for black sweaters. Though they had bought her two already, she still wanted one with *pockets*.

"You *said* we could visit the Bedouins!" Rafik's voice from the back seat was insistent. He didn't beg very often. "Please!" Khaled and Nadine jabbered in Arabic to each other.

Poppy looked at his watch. "If we visit them, we may not make it to the Dead Sea. They'll keep us all day."

"We'll just run away!"

Poppy said, "Khaled, what do you say?"

Khaled's voice was gentle. He never wanted to boss anyone around. "I say—*yes?*"

The minute Liyana's eyes focused on the flapping black tents, she noticed a small camel staked beside them, the first she'd seen in this country since they arrived. Poppy always included camels in his childhood stories and folk tales, but they'd mostly vanished from this land since then. Where had they gone? Had they all trekked away to Saudi Arabia or Abu Dhabi? She'd been wishing so hard to see one.

Liyana pitched in, "Yes! Let's visit them for just a minute! Come on, Poppy!" Nadine was laughing.

Poppy groaned, "A Bedouin's minute is an hour to you. Maybe two or three. Believe me."

But he pulled the car farther off the road. He said, "What if we get stuck in a sand dune? What if the sand shifts while we're visiting and swallows the car entirely?" But his children were relentless.

Poppy had said Bedouins, like their camels, were much fewer and farther apart than they used to be, but still as friendly. "I thought they were fierce," Rafik said.

Poppy said, "They are, but not to their guests."

The five of them hiked in toward the tents. Halfway there, Poppy returned to the car to get the basket of bananas. "You always bring a gift to Bedouins," he said. "Like a house gift. To people without a house."

The women of the tribe were off beyond the tents shaking dust from little rugs. Children in baggy clothes played a game involving sticks, balls, and large tin cans. Tall men with lean faces sat before the largest tent, wearing black cloaks and headdresses, stitching tarps together with huge needles. Maybe they were making a new tent, Liyana thought.

The camel shifted its feet as they approached. It watched them closely. Spectacular white cheeses lay lined like thirty perfect moons on a dark cloth, drying in the sun. Nadine pointed at them and babbled excitedly to Khaled. She said in English, "So much!"

All the men rose up as they approached. Poppy talked fast and heartily so that before they knew it, they were sitting in a circle with the Bedouins. Everyone was laughing and nodding and asking questions about America and the women were serving tea and slicing a cheese in front of Rafik.

He looked worried. He hated white cheese. Liyana grinned.

Poppy translated, "They're ready to adopt you. See? I told you. Get set for a long day."

He also said, "I told them we are Arab-Americans and they're shocked. They didn't know such people existed. We're the first visitors who've come by in a long time. In the old days people used to stop in more. Bedouins don't even wander as much as they used to. Nowadays they change places only once a year, instead of every few months. In

Saudi Arabia the Bedouins have all been settled in town. It's a shame. It was a great tradition."

Rafik's eyes were huge. Did the woman think he was going to eat the whole cheese? Why were they focusing on him instead of Khaled? Maybe they liked his red and blue striped T-shirt. Nadine took four pieces of cheese, which helped him out.

"How do Bedouins live?" Liyana asked Poppy. "I mean, where do they get their money?"

"Money? Do you see any money? The goats are in a patch of grass over the dune somewhere. The people sleep right here. They eat right here. Their lives are extremely simple."

Now Liyana knew. She wanted to be a Bedouin when she grew up.

A woman with kind eyes produced two goatskin drums. Even though Poppy said Bedouin music usually happened after sundown, two young men began slapping quick rhythms and singing for them—the same words and notes repeated over and over. Liyana clapped her hands and hummed along. They liked that. Nadine snapped her fingers. A girl with tight braids swayed and bent hypnotically. Khaled accepted a drum and began playing with one swift, accurate hand. Rafik leaned backward on the tarp, as far from the cheese as he could. He nodded bravely when the women pointed at it again.

They sat within the graceful slopes of dunes, tucked away from the road and the few cars and jeeps going by. Liyana felt her thoughts drifting into the sky. Her eyelids drooped. Was this music putting her into a trance? She wished her friends from back home could be here. This was what they would call "an exotic moment." She wished her mother were here, too—hermit women couldn't be more interesting than *this*.

After the ninety-ninth verse of the song, Poppy stood up. The Bedouins protested. "Please," they said to him in Arabic, "you must spend the night!" Poppy laughed. He promised they'd be back. What could they bring them from the city? The Bedouins wanted Rafik to take a cheese home with him—a new cheese, not even the strong one they had all nibbled from. Poppy left the bananas and the basket both. The Bedouins liked the basket. They kept touching it admiringly. It was her mother's favorite basket. Liyana wondered, would she be upset?

Walking back to the car with the entire Bedouin tribe sadly watching them leave, Poppy said to Rafik, "Oh no, you didn't even ride the camel! You petted it, anyway. It's their last camel. Was it too small to ride? Shall we go back? You want to try?"

Rafik considered it. He turned and waved,

looking wistful. Liyana said, "Remember, camels can spit."

Poppy sighed, "And we might have to leave you."

━━━━◆━━━━

The Dead Sea water was so prickly with salt, it stung Liyana's eyes. Her skin felt marinated after ten minutes.

"It's seven times saltier than the ocean!" Poppy called out. He strolled back and forth by the water wearing a white baseball cap pulled low over his thick hair. He hated swimming. "How do you feel at the lowest spot on earth?"

"Down deep!"

"Bottomed out!"

They were practically sitting on top of the water, as if invisible lounge chairs buoyed them up. Rafik called out, "Strange!" He was paddling fast like a duck. Khaled laughed harder than Liyana had ever seen him laugh. "Did you like the Bedouins?" she asked.

He said, "*Very* much. Did I ever tell you my *Sidi*—grandfather—was half Bedouin? Once when I was small he took me to visit, like today."

"Where is he—now?"

"He is dead. He and—my *Sitti*, too. When our village was taken away. I saw it."

"Saw what?"

"The Israeli soldiers—exploded a house. You know, like they do when they think you are bad. And the house fell on my grandparents. It was not their house."

A single puffed cloud drifted past overhead. Far away someone hooted and leapt into the sea.

"And then what? Did your family fight back?" Liyana asked. Khaled had never mentioned many personal things before.

Khaled said haltingly, "My family—does not like to fight. My parents are very—sad till now. They will never be finished with sadness. I—had a bad picture in my mind—a long time. For myself I never fight. Then my mind is sick and doesn't get well. Sadness is—better."

Liyana said, "I think I would fight. Not kill, but yell or something."

In the car going home, Liyana would tell Poppy what Khaled had told her and Poppy would ask him more questions in Arabic. For now the thick gray water seared a scrape on Liyana's knee. She said, "Khaled, nothing about this sea feels dead to me."

ALL OUR ROOTS GO DEEP DOWN EVEN IF THEY'RE TANGLED

She wanted another kiss—
her chapped lips were burning up.

In March, Poppy found three American evangelists lost in the Old City and brought them home for dinner. Liyana thought, "If I were his wife, I would say *Thanks a lot* and not mean it."

But her mother was in the kitchen humming happily and clattering pot lids as the visitors sat around the table toasting each other with glasses of mint tea and gobbling roasted chickpeas. Rafik showed them the new designs he'd been sketching for Star Trek phasers. He could tune in to planets X, Y, and Z. The two evangelist men, Reverend Crump and Reverend Holman, wore bright red-and-navy diagonally striped ties, and the woman, Reverend Walker, wore a long gray dress with a lace collar. Liyana asked the woman cautiously, "Are you married to…?" and nodded at the men, curious if one was her mate and she used her own name, but the woman declared, "Honey, I'm married to THE LORD'S GOOD WILL!"

Poppy said they had been wandering with dazed looks by the shoe shops where the streets get narrower when he stopped to offer directions. "Our countrymen!" But they didn't remind Liyana of anyone else she'd ever met in her life.

Reverend Walker said, "God told us to visit Mount Gilboa right now to see the blessed Gilboa iris that only blooms three weeks a year. So we packed our bags in Atlanta and *bought tickets! Amen!*"

Now they were waiting for further instructions from God because they hadn't received a complete itinerary. What were they supposed to do after they had visited the flowers and the Church of the Nativity and the other holy spots lined up like pearly buttons across the stony ground?

Poppy offered his advice. "I know a hospital that could really use some volunteers right now. It's in Gaza and all the orderlies have been quitting and the nurses are in an uproar and nothing is getting done. Just a day or two of help would be a—Godsend."

The evangelists looked at one another. Reverend Holman said, *"Praise the Lord!"* after Mom served the lentil soup and the coleslaw, which reminded them of home, and the stuffed grape leaves and the hot bread. But every one of them was quiet when Poppy mentioned the hospital.

Reverend Crump told Poppy he wished they could say a prayer in Hebrew for him. Poppy mentioned that he didn't know any prayers in Hebrew himself, but Liyana didn't think they got it. When Poppy went to the kitchen to get a fresh pitcher of tea, she leaned forward and said gently, "We're not Jewish, you know."

Then Reverend Walker asked Liyana if she'd been bathed in the blood of Jesus and she could see Rafik's eyes open wider. Luckily her tongue got stuck and her mother replied, "Um—we don't think—quite in those terms."

So everyone had some nut cookies and hot tea. Rafik said, out of the blue, "Do you know what our grandmother has in her collection? She has an empty tear gas canister that the Israeli soldiers threw at her house one day. It says *Made in Pennsylvania* on the side of it. The soldiers get their weapons and their money from the United States." The guests' eyes grew wide. They didn't know what to say. Then Rafik buttered his last pocket of bread.

Reverend Holman said to their mother, as if Rafik and Liyana weren't present, "Your children must feel alienated here, don't they?"

Mom said, puffing proudly, "I think they're doing quite well."

Rafik added, sighing in a melodramatic way, "But we *do* miss the school milk in little red cartons," which made his mother put her thumb and first finger together like an alligator closing its mouth.

After dinner the visitors went out on the front balcony to meditate on the hospital idea. Rafik and Liyana wrinkled their noses at each other and escaped into Rafik's room, where he put on his cassette tape of Japanese bamboo flute music. Liyana stared out the window where the heavens blazed like an orange bonfire, and wrote in her notebook:

The hills are dark with the shadows of night
But up in the sky is a brilliant light
of fire, fire, fire in the sky.

That day her geography teacher had said Arabs and Jews should trade places for a while and see what it felt like to be each other. But Atom said it would be too hard to do. She wondered. Could she even imagine exactly what it would feel like to be her own brother? Poppy's voice called them back to the living room. "We miss you in here!"

Reverend Crump asked for a last glass of water so he could take his "anti-panic pill" and Liyana stifled a laugh, pretending it was a cough. Poppy asked if the meal had upset him and he said, "Night brings on a brooding melancholia."

When Reverend Walker laid her hand on his back and said something that sounded as if she were speaking in tongues, "HIYA-hallah-wallah-kallah-mone," Rafik's eyes widened with interest.

Reverend Holman announced they'd decided to travel on into Jordan because they really wanted to see the famous carved city of Petra, so they'd better not take on any voluntary duties at that poor hospital in Gaza after all. But Lord have mercy, they'd keep it in their prayers.

Later, after he had driven them back to their hotel, Poppy was muttering, "Holy, holy, holy."

ℋABIBI

> *Darling: a dearly loved person,*
> *a favorite, a charmer.*

For years the word floated in the air around their heads, yellow pollen, wispy secret dust of the ages passed on and on.

Habibi, darling, or *Habibti*, feminine for my darling. Poppy said it before bedtime or if they fell off their bikes—as a soothing syrup, to make them feel sweetened again. He said it as good morning or tucked in between sentences. He said it when they left for school.

Whatever else happened, Liyana and Rafik were his darlings all day and they knew it. Even when he stayed at the hospital past their bedtimes, they could feel his *darling* drifting comfortably around them.

Their mother called them "precious"—her own English version of the word. She fed them, folded their clothes even when they could have done it themselves, and squeezed fresh orange juice instead of opening frozen cans.

At Liyana's house they had fresh apple salad

with dates, baked yams, delicious stir-fried cabbage. They had a father who wrapped their mother in his arms. They had "*Habibi,* be careful, *Habibti,* I love you," trailing them like a long silken scarf. Liyana knew it didn't happen for everybody.

———

In Jerusalem they were living in the land of *Habibi*—Sitti rolled it off her tongue toward them and it balanced in the air like a bubble. They hovered inside the wide interest of these people they barely knew.

Their giant family offered them glasses of cool lemonade with sprigs of mint stuck in like straws. They handed them bowls of pastel Jordan almonds and the softest cushions to sit on.

In return, Liyana's family gave them oddities to think about. Liyana played the violin for them and told them, through Poppy, she would be in a symphony in Europe someday. They didn't know what a symphony was. Liyana wore blue jeans with paisley patches on the knees and her aunts pointed and whispered.

Poppy admonished her, "They think you're destitute if you dress like that."

Liyana said, "So?" She repeated the word inside her mind. "Des-ti-tute. Desti-TOOT." She started to like it.

Liyana smashed a potato in a bowl, mixed it with butter, milk, and salt till it was creamy, and offered it to Sitti. *"Mashed potato,"* she said, as Sitti carefully tasted it, and smiled. Sitti took the whole bowl from her hands and gobbled it down. She even tried to shape the words. *"Mash bo-tay-toes."*

It was the first English she'd ever tried to say.

Liyana's whole family seemed to be joining things. Poppy had joined a human-rights group to focus on treatment and services for old people. Rafik had joined an ecology club at his school—they would work with garbage and recycling. Their mother belonged to a Women's Communications Club—women of different backgrounds writing letters to editors and sharing optimistic ideas. She would probably be elected president soon. After their first meeting, the *Jerusalem Post* wrote an editorial saying if other people followed their example, the peace process might zoom ahead.

And Liyana? She belonged to nothing but Watchers Anonymous. She walked the streets of old Jerusalem muttering her new words in Arabic, sprinkling them down into cracks between stones. *Ana tayyib*—I'm fine. *Wa alaykum essalaam*—and upon you peace. *Shway*—a little bit. Watermelon was *hubhub*. It wasn't any harder to say *Ana asif*—I'm sorry—than it was to say other things.

But people acted like it was. Two taxi drivers honked and honked at a jammed intersection, refusing to budge. A boy threw a hard ball at a geranium pot on Imm Janan's front step and it shattered.

Liyana was no better. One day in Arabic class she grew so irritated with the dull text, she ripped a whole page out of her book. The teacher ordered her to stand in the hall and wrote a mean letter to her father. In Arabic.

Poppy said, *"Habibti, please."*

Liyana took a walk by herself down by the refugee camp, standing for a long time in the pinkish light soaking up the quiet motions of evening. Women unpinned skirts and undershirts from lines. Where were Nadine and Khaled tonight? She always felt better when she talked to them. Boys polished crooked bicycles with rags. What pumped up their hopes?

"Poppy, do you think there will ever be a time when all people get along just fine?" she asked when she got home.

He was marking hospital charts at the table.

"Nope."

What would Liyana do if she could?

She'd touch Omer's shoulder lightly and leave a little *habibi* dust there. She'd place one secret red poppy alongside Sitti's pillow and disappear into the cool night air.

ℬANANA EASTER

Who can guess
what the weather will bring?

Jerusalem woke to a blizzard for the first time in fifty years on Easter Sunday. Poppy stood by the front window exclaiming, "This is just not something you expect to see here!"

The road out front looked strangely deserted except for a few kids in raggedy jackets and two disoriented goats. Rafik ran downstairs in his pajamas, opening his mouth to the sky. He said the snow tasted like icing without vanilla in it.

Mrs. Abboud had tried to bake hot cross buns, as she did every Easter, but they didn't rise. "Let's call them hot cross pancakes," she said. It was the first year nobody was interested in hiding any eggs.

The whole family drove slowly through swirling snow to the Garden Tomb, where Liyana's mother wanted to attend the sunrise service. She got ideas into her head and would not let go of them, no matter what the weather. How could she miss her first Easter service here in the place where everything had really *happened?* Arab families stood outside in their transformed yards staring happily up into the magical air. Did they even know how to make snowballs?

Recently, Liyana's mother had narrated a program at the radio station called "Debate Over the Tombs." Some people believed the tomb of Jesus was at a different location. Mom voted for the one on the cliff above the bus station, a cave in the craggy rock, where a small group of devout and frozen people was already waiting, shivering in skinny coats and scarves and hats and gloves.

The sun did not rise.

Or if it rose, no one could tell.

There was snow on the crooked branches of the olive tree. People crowded close among snow-capped stones while a priest with chattering teeth held his Bible and tried to speak. He said Easter gave human beings their highest hopes. It was the "greatest feast of the year, the victory march of the human soul." Poppy leaned over to whisper in Liyana's ear, "Jerusalem needs lower hopes, too; down-to-the-ground, pebble-sized, poppy-seed-sized hopes." She closed her eyes, trying to feel what it *meant* to be assured that dying did not just mean *dead.*

Many in the crowd were weeping. Maybe they had dreamed of being here for years. Maybe they had traveled from Spain and California and the tears would freeze on their cheeks. Near the end of the service, a tall, thin-faced lady toppled over backward into the snow and struck Liyana with her elbow on the way down. Rafik blurted, "Whoa!"

Poppy rushed to the lady's side. He carried smelling salts in his pocket for such occasions. He carried aspirins and nitroglycerin tablets and who knew what else. He leaned over and spoke to the fallen lady gently. She didn't seem very hurt. She kept arranging her hair. Poppy took her pulse and whispered to her while someone called a taxi to drive her back to her hotel. She said she didn't need to go to a hospital and that she fainted every time she got "emotional."

She had disrupted the final prayer. As a few Americans started singing "How Great Thou Art," to fill in the space, Liyana's eyes traveled curiously around the group. She felt startled to see her secretly famous banana seller standing off to the right, wearing a bulky blue sweater much too large for him. He'd been hidden behind someone till people began moving around. His hands were poked up high in either sleeve. Liyana had never seen him without his cart before. She poked Rafik and whispered, "Look who's here!"

Poppy helped the weak-kneed lady into the

car, then turned to Liyana as it disappeared. He was grinning. "You know what? She thought this snow was a miracle—it swept her away!"

Behind Poppy, the dwarf broke into the first smile Liyana had ever seen on his face. He said, in Arabic, *"Mabruk"*—"Congratulations!"

Liyana reached toward him to shake his hand.

"Fee mooz?" she asked, which meant something like, "Do you have a banana?" Or maybe it meant, *"Is there* a banana?" which sounded a little foolish if you considered it.

Miraculously, as miraculous as snow on Easter and strangers passing out onto the ground, the small, smiling man pulled a stubby banana from his pants pocket and handed it to her. She tried to press a coin from her wallet into his hand, but he waved it away, laughing heartily, saying Arabic words she couldn't understand.

Poppy looked startled by this odd transaction. "What's going on?" he said.

Liyana dangled her prize banana in front of his nose. A yellow banana in the white, white snow.

Rafik said, "It's an Easter egg."

𝒜 DAY
COULD UNFOLD

Teach me to sew a vine of stars.

One day at lunchtime, after buying a slightly tattered two-months-old American women's magazine at the newsstand as a surprise for her mother, Liyana heard her name floating above the idling taxis near the King David Hotel. She raised her head to the sky as if a bird had called her.

Then Omer appeared, sprinting up to her startled side, and said, "You didn't tell me your name means a vine! I found it spelled almost the same way in the dictionary—a tropical rain- forest vine. It roots in the ground."

Liyana grinned. "Where have you *been?*"

"Where have *you* been?"

He said, "I was going to call you last night." It seemed like a thin little lie anybody might say, but she liked it.

Omer wanted to invite her to a poetry reading by local poets at his school that evening. She said she'd have to see if one of her parents could drive her, since it was at night. He drew a map to his school on the back of a grocery list written in Hebrew from his pocket.

"Do you still have my number?" he asked.

Liyana thought, *Oh please.*

"Well," he grinned, "you did not use it recently, so I could not be sure."

He held her elbow for a moment before she ran off toward the Armenian Quarter and her Arabic class, which was already two minutes into its lesson on how to ask questions.

Again, as it had before when Liyana saw Omer at lunchtime, the afternoon puffed up lightly, joyously, a delicate pastry, a sweetened shell of hours.

On the local bus home, everything still shone in the light of Omer's smile. The cracked bus seats, squealing brakes, ladies with huge plastic bags of fresh bread, the bus driver's bald head, were shining, shining.

"Shookran!" Liyana exclaimed to the driver, climbing down at her stop. *"Thank you!"*

She was not usually so enthusiastic.

The driver lifted his hands from the wheel and shimmied them in the air, laughing at her. *"Alham'dul-Allah!"*

Praise be to God—that a day could unfold with surprise invitations. Liyana leapt upstairs two steps at a time.

But she was met by her brother with a stunned look on his face. "Khaled's been shot," he said. "And Poppy's in jail."

HOW MANY SIDES DOES A STORY HAVE?

A story is a seam in a dress—
some days it unravels.

"What?" screamed Liyana. "What do you mean? Where is Mom?"

She dropped her school bag onto the floor.

"Mom went off in a Palestinian police car. She made me stay here to tell you. She is *very very* upset." Rafik looked bleary-eyed.

"How do these things go together?"

"What things?"

"Khaled and Poppy!"

"I don't know," he sobbed. "I'm telling you everything she told me. Ismael's father dropped me off here after school and Mom was blazing out the door into a police car that was parked out back, this strange kind of car I don't even know the name of, and I didn't get any more details."

"ALWAYS get details!"

Liyana rushed into the kitchen and stared at the phone. She had no idea whom to call. In this country you didn't call 911. "Let's go down to the camp and find Nadine," she said. "Maybe Nadine can tell us something."

Liyana and Rafik galloped down the road without speaking. The refugee camp looked more topsy-turvy than usual. Beat-up cars sat at odd angles out front, as if people had jumped from them without parking. A sack of pita bread lay scattered on the ground. A heap of smoking rubber tires polluted the air. And a crowd of teenaged boys huddled together by the small house with the blue-painted front door where Khaled and Nadine lived with their parents.

"Hello!" Liyana shouted to the boys. "Please, *wane* Nadine?"

The boys yelled in unison, "Nadine!"

Nadine came to her window and peered out anxiously.

"*Yallah!*" Liyana yelled to her. "Quickly! We need to talk to you!"

Nadine came stepping out of the house with bare feet. She was shivering. Where were her shoes? Where was her shy mother, Abla, who often served small plates of delicious sweets and figs to Liyana and Rafik?

"Where is your mother?" Liyana said.

Nadine cried, "She went hospital with Khaled. He was bad, bad! Shot!"

"We heard that! It's terrible! But—who shot him?"

Nadine said the word for "soldiers" and covered her eyes.

Liyana stared at Rafik, baffled. "So how did Poppy get into this?" Of course she had never considered that their father, who could not even trap a mouse, had shot their friend, but the connections seemed jumbled.

"You father—he come run—from you house," explained Nadine. "He see the soldiers—no like it. He come run, he wave arms," she demonstrated, waving wildly. "The soldiers call *Khaled!—come out house!* Khaled no come out." She used the Arabic word for "scared." She was crying hard now. "The soldiers say, *Yallah! Yallah!* The soldiers mad! Khaled come out, turn round and the soldier shoot! Khaled fall down. Is bad, bad! You father run to soldier, say *No! No!* He stop him." She threw her arm.

Liyana was staring open-mouthed.

Rafik said, "He *hit* the soldier?"

"No, no, no hit, just…" She showed them. Poppy had pulled the soldier's arm back. Hard.

Liyana covered her mouth. Rafik asked, "The arm that had a gun in it?" but Nadine didn't understand. Nadine said the ambulance came for Khaled and the soldiers took Poppy. They pushed him into a car.

Now everybody was crying. Liyana was crying. "Which hospital?" she wailed. "And where is the jail?"

One of Khaled's cousins knew where the jail was. He'd been in it twice himself. He didn't look very happy about going back there. But he walked quickly with Liyana and Rafik to the Abbouds' house to call a taxi.

When they reached Jerusalem, after passing the usual daily things—vegetable carts, sheep, stores, family vineyards propped on poles—the taxi turned sharply onto a gray industrial-looking street.

At the grim-faced jail, Liyana strode up to three Israeli soldiers guarding the front and said, "Please, I need to see my father, Dr. Kamal Abboud. He hasn't been here long. He came— maybe an hour ago."

One soldier sitting on a crate lifted his eyes sleepily from the orange he was peeling. "Not possible," he said. She could smell the fragrant orange scent rising from his hands.

Something shifted inside her. It trembled and

could have turned her away. Her throat felt shaky. But she didn't turn. She stomped her foot on the pavement, raising her leg twice and pounding her foot down as hard as she could. Liyana stomped her foot at the soldiers. "Of *course* it's possible!" she said loudly. "He is my *father!* I need to see him! NOW! PLEASE! It's necessary! I must go in this minute!"

The soldiers looked her up and down. She was still wearing her navy blue school uniform with its rumpled white cotton blouse. The soldier with the orange sighed heavily, as if she were really irritating him. He dropped the peelings into a sack, wiped his hands, and said, "Come." But another soldier put his arm up and made Rafik stay out front, which made him furious.

———

The first soldier took Liyana into an office, shone a hot spotlight into her face, and photographed her. He asked her name, age, school, her phone number, and address, barking his questions. He asked two more times what she wanted and she repeated, "To see my father." Did he have a bad memory? The second time she spoke calmly and slowly. He took the embroidered purse Sitti had made and said she could not take it in. She watched him toss it onto a dirty table cluttered with empty coffee cups. He said she could not stay long.

Liyana followed the soldier down a gloomy hall, staring into dark cells as her eyes adjusted. Sleeping bodies lay wrapped in blankets on cots. Some cubicles had high slits for windows, but some had none. One man stood tall in the center of his cell, staring straight toward the hall where she walked, his hands held behind his back. His face looked blank. It was strange to walk through a jail. What were the prisoners' stories? How long had they been here? Had they done anything worse than her father had?

Poppy sat on a wooden stool in a cell bent over with his head in his hands. Usually he only sat this way when one of his patients was dying. Her mother was nowhere to be seen. A small moan escaped from Poppy's mouth when he saw her through the iron bars, but he wasn't crying. The air smelled dank and sour.

"*Habibti!*" he said. "*No no no!* What in the world are you doing here? How did you get in? This is no place for you!"

"Or you either," Liyana said, gripping a bar. It was strange how calm she felt the minute she entered his presence. "Poppy! We have to help you get out!"

He said, "I'm working on it. Liyana, don't

worry. I'll be out soon. It's a big mistake. Take care of yourself! *Go home! Stay safe!*" The soldier stood behind Liyana with his arms folded.

"Where is your mother?"

"I don't know! I thought she might be here. How bad is Khaled? Which hospital is he in?"

Poppy thought Khaled's leg wound would not kill him. "It was low down. I hope they wrapped it before he bled much. The soldiers whisked me away so I couldn't even help him! I kept telling them I was a doctor! I said, "Since when do you arrest doctors on the scene of an injury?" But they wouldn't listen to me. Oh, it certainly was a case of being in the wrong place at the wrong time. I know you hate that phrase." He shook his head. "I just keep thinking how we used to carve faces into acorns with our pocket knives. We would stick broken matches into them and spin them on the ground like tops. Now look where we are!" He waved his hand back and forth as if to indicate he was speaking about all the prisoners on the hall. And the soldiers too.

"But Poppy, what was *happening* at the camp in the first place?" Liyana asked.

He said, "*Habibti,* if I wanted to talk about first places, I'd have to go too far back. What was happening *today* was the bomb in the Jewish marketplace—did you hear about the bomb?—near a school, which is terrible. The soldiers got a tip that someone in Khaled's camp had something to do with it. That's why they came into territory they're not supposed to be administering anymore. Maybe they thought Khaled did it! But we *know* how much Khaled hates violence....How could I stand by saying nothing? He's not a bathtub, for God's sake...."

The soldier stepped forward roughly, motioning that he was ready to escort Liyana out, but she held her hand up and said sternly, "WAIT." Poppy opened his dark eyes very wide. He raised his eyebrows. "Liyana, go!" he ordered. "Get out of here!"

The man in the next cell was praying loudly.

"Poppy, *we love you!*" she said, clinging to the bars with both hands by now. She could have thrown herself down on the ground like a little girl having a tantrum. But she held back, held tightly, saying only, "This is not *right.*"

Poppy placed two fingers on his lips and blew a kiss at her. "Don't tell Sitti!" he said. "Promise me! She'll stage a revolution! Take care, *habibti!* And where's Rafik?" he shouted, as the guard marched her off.

"Outside! They wouldn't let him in!"

Liyana reclaimed her purse from the office and asked the soldier if he knew where her mother might be, but he pretended he didn't understand her.

Before jumping back into the waiting taxi with Rafik and Khaled's cousin, who both looked deeply curious about what had just happened inside the jail, Liyana stared hard into the face of the soldier who had escorted her. He was sitting on his crate again. She didn't blink. She wanted to see him clearly.

Then she stared into the faces of the other two soldiers guarding the prison door. They leaned into the wall, huge guns slung over their shoulders. They could have been handsome if they had smiled. She couldn't stop herself. Pointing at them with the forefingers of both her hands, she said loudly, "You do not have to be so mean! You could be nicer! My father is a doctor! My friend you shot is a gentle person! YOU DO NOT HAVE TO BE THIS WAY!"

The soldiers didn't say anything. But they looked surprised.

At the tall white hospital, which reeked of ammonia, but still smelled better than the jail, Liyana, Rafik, and Khaled's cousin were admitted to see Khaled without any trouble. Liyana and Rafik said they were his cousins, too. They let the true cousin do the talking until they got inside.

Khaled was still down in Emergency on a thin

little bed with his leg wrapped as tightly as a stuffed grape leaf. His mother sat beside him wringing water out of a washcloth. She was bathing his face. Khaled looked surprised to see his visitors and lifted partway up on his elbows.

"What!" he said weakly. "You find me! I am worried about your father! Where is he?"

A nurse refreshed a water glass beside Khaled's bed. She stared at his guests, then left. Khaled said he'd heard about the bomb on the radio and felt very sad. Then he said, "You know I know nothing else about it."

"We know."

Rafik stared at Liyana. *She* knew. He didn't know. He hated being cut out of things. Liyana said they'd both seen Nadine, who was very upset. She said Poppy was acting fairly calm behind bars. Khaled shook his head. "He was good to me. He tried to stop them. He hates fighting, too. He told me that when we came home from the Dead Sea. I can't believe they took him!"

"Doesn't this make you feel *more* like fighting?" Liyana asked.

Khaled sighed heavily, stretching his upper body as if his neck were stiff. He seemed very tired. "Believe me, I feel less. Ohhhhh..." He closed his eyes and sighed. "Did you know—it's my birthday?"

"NO!" Liyana and Rafik spoke together. "Is it really?"

Rafik shook his head soberly. "I'm starting to think birthdays are bad luck."

A black-and-white clock on the wall said six. The fragrance of cooking rice wafted down the hospital hall. At least *some* things still felt normal.

As they exited the hospital, Rafik said, "*Now* where are we going?"

Liyana whispered, "Home."

———

She liked how the taxi driver waited wherever they asked him to. He was idling in front of the hospital. He knew they were having an upsetting day. In the car heading north, Rafik said, "Tell me every one of Poppy's words. Did he look scared? Did they have chains in there?"

Liyana said, "I didn't see chains," but Khaled's cousin, the one who had been in jail himself, said, "Believe me, they have everything."

It seemed strange to find their house sitting calmly where it always sat, lights in the first-floor windows and the upstairs dark. Their car was still parked outside, too. But their mother wasn't back yet. She rang them up from police headquarters in Jerusalem soon after they had entered the house and flicked on lights in every room.

"I have good news," she reported, brightly. "They say your father will be released tonight. I haven't seen him. I've been filling out papers in ten offices. This is the worst day of my life, but it will have a happy ending! Have you been home all afternoon?"

———

Liyana went downstairs to ask Abu Janan more about the bomb in the market. He shook his head. "People dead." Old men and women. Innocent, everyday people who had as much to do with politics as Liyana did. Shopping bags. Corn. Purses. Stockings. Shoes. Kleenex. Teeth. Earrings.

How could anyone do that? Liyana thought. Maybe it was done by the Arab father whose ten-year-old son was shot by Israeli soldiers last week. Maybe it was done by the brothers of the tortured prisoners Poppy met all the time, or the cousin of the mayor who lost both legs when the Israelis blew up his car. Did people who committed acts of violence think their victims and their victims' relatives would just *forget?*

Didn't people see? How violence went on and on like a terrible wheel? Could you stand in front of a wheel to make it stop? What if Khaled had been killed when he was shot? Would that have made Liyana or Nadine do something violent, too? It was better, as happened with Khaled's own grandparents and himself, if you were able to let the violence stop when it got to you. But many people couldn't do that.

———

The telephone rang in their apartment again and Rafik raced up the stairs to get it. "It's for you!" he shouted down to Liyana.

Her feet felt leaden on the stairs.

"Poetry reading?" Omer's voice said.

Liyana had forgotten completely.

NEGOTIATIONS

Maybe peace was the size of a teacup.

"Jail," said Poppy soberly, settling himself on the couch with a large glass of water and tipping his head back, "is an experience I don't ever want to have again." He'd come home from jail at 11 P.M. in a taxi and the driver refused to take a cent from him.

Liyana, Rafik, and their mother were shocked when Sitti climbed out of the taxi after him. Where did *she* come from? Rafik and Liyana jumped up and down. "Poppy's home! Poppy's free!" He hugged them so tightly, Liyana felt surprised.

Sitti had appeared at the jail a few hours after Liyana did. The soldiers wouldn't let her in, though. As Poppy was being released, he found her outside shouting, waving a broom, and demanding to see the governor. "She still thinks it's fifty years ago," he said, shaking his head. "We had someone called a governor then." An old lady she knew at Khaled's camp had called Sitti's village to tell about Poppy being arrested.

Poppy said, "You can't keep any secrets over here."

———

A few nights later the Abbouds were eating cabbage rolls at the dinner table—Mom made Liyana a small casserole of vegetarian ones on the side, filled with nuts and raisins and rice—and everything was almost back to normal. Khaled was back at the camp with a heavily bandaged leg and a crutch. The Abbouds had been down to welcome him with molasses cookies that afternoon. Sitti had carried her broom home to its corner.

But Poppy seemed a little odd. He'd taken a few days off from work and kept sitting at the dining table scribbling notes and staring into space. He made an unusual number of phone calls and spoke only in Arabic. One day their mother reported he wore his pajama top till noon—something he *never* did.

When Liyana asked what was going on, he said he couldn't stop thinking about all the people who were still in jail—many for more ridiculous reasons than his own. He was becoming an activist in his old age. He was going to see the Jewish mayor of Jerusalem tomorrow. He'd heard a man coughing too hard a few cells down. The man obviously needed medicine. He put both his hands up in the air. He walked down to the refugee camp and talked to everybody. He rolled his papers and banged them on the table. "I'm trying to figure out how many things an ordinary citizen can do!"

But at dinner he asked Liyana, "Now what are *you* thinking about? The tables are turned. You've been so quiet tonight."

She dove in. "Could my friend Omer—Mom's met him—come to the village with us someday soon? He's never been to—an Arab village. He invited me to a poetry reading the other evening, but I wasn't able to go, since my father was just getting out of jail—so I thought it might be nice to invite him somewhere, too."

Poppy's hand went up to his forehead. "Right now? Oh, Liyana. He's curious about us? He wants to know how we do things? He likes our food?"

"You don't have to sound so defensive!"

Poppy was silent for a moment. That's what *he* always said to *her*. "Our family—wouldn't appreciate it. They wouldn't—understand. It would seem suspicious—or unsettling to them. The peace isn't stabilized enough yet."

"Understand? What's there to understand about having a friend?"

"Liyana—you know. You're just acting innocent on purpose."

"I *don't* know! I don't *want* to know! What good is it to believe in peace and talk about peace if you only want to live the same old ways?"

"Is his family orthodox?"

"No. He doesn't seem orthodox—anything. He seems very universal."

Poppy sighed. "They always seem—universal. Do you have any passages from your favorite prophet Kahlil Gibran you'd like to read to me just now?"

Liyana's mother tapped her water glass with a spoon. "Don't make fun," she said to Poppy. "Remember what my parents said when I fell in love with you? They said nothing, remember? And do you remember how cruel that was?"

Poppy reeled back in his chair. "Now she's in love?" he thundered. "Liyana's in love? I thought she just wanted to go to the village!"

Rafik was roaring. Liyana hated this.

"So is it okay or not?" she asked, pushing back two lonely green beans to the edge of her plate.

Poppy was quiet.

A bus roared by on the road outside.

Liyana said softly, "We want to write a new story," and Poppy said, "What?"

Mom, queen of her Communications Club, took a deep breath. "She's right, you know. What good is a belief in peace if it doesn't change the ways we live?"

But Poppy wasn't listening. "It's *inappropriate* for a girl to invite a boy anywhere in this part of the world. They'll think you're engaged or something. They'll think he's a spy. How will I explain him?"

Rafik groaned. "Could we talk about something else? Let's just invite him already! Who cares? Say he's MY FRIEND, not Liyana's! Say he's my mentor or something—like we had in school in the United States. I met him at the library. He's a nice guy. And Sitti invites everyone *else* on earth to our dinners—why not him, too? "

Liyana loved Rafik with all her heart.

Poppy said, "He was at the library, too?"

Then he said, "You're *stubborn*, dear Liyana. You're that fine Arabian horse again, constantly trying to get your own way. Why do you want to take him and not Khaled or Nadine?"

"Let's take them as well! Let's take everybody! Don't you want a coming-out party? And didn't you mention, last week, how wonderful it was when Mr. Hamadi, your favorite thousand-year-old patient, let the Jewish doctor work on his eyes and never once referred to his ethnicity? Didn't you say before you went in jail that it would be great if people never described each other as 'the Jew' or 'the Arab' or 'the black guy' or 'the white guy'—didn't you just SAY?"

Her mother repeated, "She's right, you know."

＊

After dinner, Liyana was on the phone. Omer always laughed when she identified herself with both her names. "You think I can't tell? I told you you're the only Liyana I know!" His rich voice rang out, a rippling stream of energy across the wire between their rooms. The minute she heard him, she wished they could talk forever.

Poppy had told Liyana they shouldn't "set the date" for the village trip yet. He made it sound like a marriage. It would happen—"someday"—when the time felt better. When Khaled's leg was stronger. "Don't rush me," Poppy said. "Don't rush anything. Okay?"

Omer was so happy Liyana had taken his interest seriously.

But he called her back the next day, sounding downcast, just needing to talk. His mother didn't want him to go to the village with Liyana, *ever*, but he told his mother it was very important. "Then she took a long walk," he said.

"What does that mean?"

"It means she's worried. And I'm going. Just let me know when."

Omer was leaving for two weeks with his class on an extended field trip to a kibbutz in northern

Israel. They did this every year. He wasn't thrilled about it. He'd be picking cherries, boxing them, digging, and weeding. The thought of such a long gap till they might meet again made Liyana's heart sputter in her throat.

She wrote for two hours that night, putting the word "heart" together with every verb she could think of. Her heart tipped, it rumbled, it swelled. She tried to write a story in which she was not the main character, in which some person she had never heard of before did things and felt things. But she still had trouble imagining lives she had not lived.

NEW COUNTRY, OLD COUNTRY

For the first time these days,
she also felt like part of a sea.

When Liyana considered the echoes bouncing off the walls of Jerusalem, she felt like the dot on an *i* in an American alphabet book for babies. Nearly invisible.

When she turned a corner in the Old City, she was just a ripple of an ancient, continuing echo. *Going, going…almost gone.*

———

"Will we ever go home?" she asked Poppy after an evening walk up to the small grocery to smell the air and buy new wooden clothespins and a box of loose tea.

Poppy was whistling, so she figured it was a good moment to ask something like that.

He paused. "I would hope," he said, "that you felt comfortable here."

"Oh I *do*," she said. "I feel more comfortable every day. But I was just…wondering. Sometimes

I get incredibly homesick for…"

Then her mind went blank. What was she really homesick for? Those ugly green signs marking exits off the interstate? The sports sections of American newspapers that she never glanced at anyway? The chilled tapioca puddings in little tubs at the supermarket?

What was she really missing anymore?

———◆———

Rafik told everybody he didn't miss anything. He had too much to think about over here to waste time with missing. He also said his Arabic was developing more quickly than Liyana's because he was less afraid of making mistakes. One day Liyana was trying to say "Excuse me" to somebody and she said something like "monkey's heart."

The sea. One wave running into another. But they had lived beside the Mississippi River, not beside a sea. She used to imagine the river running southward to pour into the Gulf of Mexico she'd never visited. Now, from this great distance, she felt closer to everything than she ever had before.

She did not feel like a foreigner in the Old City anymore. Now she had her own landmarks and scenes to remember. She had Hani, the banana seller, Bilal, the fabric seller, and Bassam, the spice man. She knew where a certain stone corner was chipped away. Maybe a vendor had bumped it with his cart long ago. She knew where the cabbages were lined on burlap in front of a radiant old woman who raised one hand to Liyana as if she were blessing her. She knew the blind shopkeeper who sat on a stool in front of his shop nodding and saying, "*Sabah-al-khair*—Good morning"— to the air. The Old City was inside her already.

———

"Did you ever think," Poppy said, "that some of us might stay and some of us go back—in the future, maybe, when you and Rafik are grown? Wouldn't it be strange if you were the one who stayed—and the rest of us moved back to the States? How can anyone know what the next day brings?"

———

The next day brought two good things. One, Liyana received a tiny present in the mail from Peachy Helen, a new four-inch-tall edition of Kahlil Gibran, and it was a volume she didn't have yet. Secondly, Mr. Berberian brought up the history of the "peace talks" at school, and suggested the students ask their elders' opinions about them.

Since Liyana's family was going out to eat *kousa,* stuffed zucchini squash, in the village that evening, she got Poppy to ask Sitti at dinnertime.

Sitti was wrapping the cooked *kousa* in white cotton towels to keep them hot on the plate.

Sitti looked surprised. She puffed up like a dove when it ruffles its feathers.

She pointed at her own chest and said, "I never lost my peace inside."

$\mathscr{E}$XPEDITION

> *Her father always told them*
> *the Arabs were famous for their hospitality.*

Finally one day when Poppy was in an especially good mood because a new wing at the hospital had just been completed and his dear old patients got to move into better rooms, he said to Liyana, "Okay, why don't you invite your friends? We'll go out to the village next Saturday as usual. The Jews and Arabs are talking better over in Hebron for a change. Maybe it's a good time for—your friend—to come along. And I'd like to get Khaled and Nadine out of that camp for a day."

On Saturday, Liyana kept watching from the balcony till the lumbering bus that carried Omer appeared on the hill. She ran out to meet him. He waved happily. He said he'd liked the bus trip north, which he'd never taken before. "Not understanding all the talk around me, but just picking up bits and pieces, made me feel—free."

"I guess I should be feeling free all the time, then."

Liyana's mother walked daintily down the

steps with her hand extended. "Hello again!" she said to Omer. She was wearing her pink embroidered Mexican blouse, which she usually wore on birthdays and holidays. Liyana had even dressed up in a maroon velvet vest.

Poppy was in the bathroom when they went upstairs, "shaving," Mom said. Liyana guessed he was really hiding out. "We'll be going to the village as soon as he's ready."

Rafik lay on his bed reading a recently arrived tome of Star Trek wisdom, the Vulcan dictionary. One of his strange extraterrestrial friends in the U.S. had sent it to him. Rafik told Omer, "It took a month for it to arrive surface mail, which means it came on a ship. Liyana says it was obviously not a spaceship."

Rafik mumbled some gobbledygook to Omer that probably meant "comrade." Then he stood up, extended his hand normally, and asked in English if Omer would like to play catch until they left.

When Poppy emerged from the bathroom, his skin looked raw. He came toward Omer with his hand out, a little too jauntily, and said, "Let's hit the road!" Liyana thought he looked at Omer curiously, in a good way. They picked up Khaled and Nadine at the camp. Nadine had a bundle of *za'tar* breads wrapped in a cloth for Sitti from her mother.

Driving up to the village, Rafik and Nadine, who were smallest in size, huddled on the floor of the back seat, laughing. Liyana was tucked into the center of the seat between Khaled and Omer. Today she didn't mind at all that they were crowded. She even liked the curves more than usual, when they made her lean in Omer's direction.

Poppy stopped at three different shops to pick up newspapers, bottled water, tins of apricot juice, a stack of two dozen pita breads, a bulging sack of fresh oranges, some with leaves still attached, and a special kind of white cheese. "Keep going, already!" Liyana's mother said. "The car is stuffed!"

Liyana thought Poppy was trying to stall.

As their car careened past a concrete Jewish settlement with its enclosures of barbed-wire fencing and military tower, Omer craned his neck to stare out the window and spoke soberly. "I have never before seen this part of the West Bank. I always wanted to see it."

He stared out at stony orchard terraces and banks of olive trees. Deep pools of shade. Cradled valleys. Flocks of stone-colored sheep. Poppy kept taking full breaths at the wheel, as if he were hyperventilating. Khaled had his face pressed to the window. Omer said, "These lands don't seem abandoned. The villages look very old. I *knew* it wasn't true."

Poppy said, "Who says they are abandoned?"

Omer said, "People—say."

Then Poppy asked Omer, "What do your friends think about the West Bank?"

Khaled looked at him. Omer stared and stared out the window. He said, "They feel—scared. They—don't know. They never came here. They think it is a different world."

There was a long silence in which Poppy echoed him, whispering, "Different world?" He didn't sound mad about it.

"I never imagined it—so beautiful over here," Omer whispered.

Liyana tapped her mother on the shoulder, speaking softly. "Remember? That's just what we said!"

Rafik whispered, "Are we in a spy zone or something? Why is everybody whispering?"

Liyana's hand brushed Omer's on the seat. He gave it a little squeeze.

———

Poppy changed the subject. "Has Liyana ever told you about when I met the actor Omar Sharif?"

Omer said, "Yes, but you could tell me again." Poppy laughed. He was loosening up.

In the village, the almond trees around Sitti's house had burst wide open with fragrant white blossoms. They hadn't been blooming the week before. Everyone breathed deeply and stretched as they stepped out of the car.

Swirls of children appeared around them. They carried blue marbles, rattles in an old tin can. Their faces hoped, *did you bring us anything? Gum, candies, what, what, what?* The only cow in town, hidden within a neighbor's courtyard, let out a loud *Mooooooooo.*

Omer said, "Even the cows welcome you?"

"Of course!" Liyana said, and Poppy laughed.

Poppy pulled a handful of clinky loose change from his pocket and dropped it on the ground in front of three boys. "Oh-oh!" he shrugged, teasing them in Arabic. "Take it, take it!"

Rafik produced a pack of Chiclet chewing gum and peeled the wrapper back. He held out the box. Omer startled Liyana by pulling a plastic sack of orange balloons from the backpack he carried.

"What else do you have in there?" she asked.

He tipped his head and looked secretive. "Slowly!" he told her.

Around their heads, in the sweetness of a breeze

that already smelled of summer, a dozen children blew up their blazing orange bananas and planets. They huffed and giggled. Some had almost no air in their little lungs at all. Khaled helped them. Sitti stepped from her stone courtyard flapping her hands. She hated it when people stood around outside. She wanted them inside, sitting down. Sometimes the village felt like a kingdom with Sitti as the queen.

They stepped carefully over the crooked threshold of Sitti's house. Liyana liked watching Omer notice things. When his eyes fell on her own second-grade school picture with two missing front teeth poked into the corner of Sitti's picture frame, he pointed and made a question mark with his hand. *You?* She grinned. Balloons were bumping and plummeting against the ceiling as children batted them high.

Dareen, Liyana's second cousin ten times removed, appeared with a huge bouquet of mint. Omer stuck his face into it as she passed and she laughed. She was shy.

"I like *n'an'a*," he said, using the Arabic word for mint, which startled Liyana.

"You know some Arabic?"

He turned his finger in the air. "Language is one tiny shiny key!"

She felt a sudden regret—she didn't know

anything in Hebrew yet. "All I know is *shalom*."

"That's a beginning," Omer said. Liyana thought how both Hebrew and Arabic came from such a deep, related place in the throat. English felt skinny beside them.

But if she tried to take on one more language, she thought, she might explode—like the almond trees with their billowy blossoms.

Sitti kissed Nadine and Khaled on both cheeks and leaned down to place her hand gently on Khaled's leg. She said a blessing over it. Then she shook Omer's hand, putting her face very close to his to stare at him. Moments later, she spilled her high-pitched siren again. Was she *that* glad to see them? Flapping her fabulous tongue way back in her mouth, she wailed and trilled.

Liyana said, "I couldn't make that sound for a hundred sheckels," and Omer clapped his hands. "I saw it in an Arab movie once! It's like the tongue is trying to fly!"

———

Liyana, Rafik, and their three friends decided to hike around the village. They walked slowly because Khaled was still limping, passing the post office and climbing among the cemetery with its unmarked graves. Poppy's father's bones lay somewhere in there. Maybe he was dust. They walked among the lentil fields to a mysterious mounded shrine encircled by large smooth stones. They all stooped and looked. Prayer rugs were rolled against one wall. A circle of half-burned candles in blackened glasses filled a corner. Nadine and Rafik crawled inside. Khaled sat on a stone to rest.

Liyana plucked the feathered head from a weed. "Omer, how old were you when your father died?"

"Five."

"How did he die?"

"A car accident."

"Do you remember him?"

"He's—cloudy in my mind." He paused. Then he spoke again, staring at Khaled. "My father did not think Arabs and Jews could ever get together again. My mother says that, too, when she reads the news. She's pretty upset today. That I came here. My father thought our break was—really broken."

Khaled looked off across the valley. "It's a bad story."

Liyana said, "That's why we need to write a *better* one."

Far away, a single donkey brayed. The note resounded through the valley.

Omer ran his hand through his hair and

continued, "Sometimes I try to think of my father's eyes still in the world, looking. What did he see? He needed to see more!"

Khaled said, "We all need to see more."

They were quiet, suspended in yellow light that falls onto hills when no one is watching.

Then Rafik broke the spell, galloping down the road toward the spring where he and Omer scooped cold water straight into their palms. They splashed their own faces. They splashed each other's faces. Liyana walked behind more slowly with Khaled and Nadine. They seemed a little sad. Khaled said, "We wish our family lived up *here*."

Later everyone washed their hands and sat on floor cushions in the big family circle as platters of steaming food traveled around. They scooped mounds of rice and cauliflower onto plates and Omer asked questions through Poppy. He wanted to know people's jobs, how they were connected. Poppy said, "Don't get started! They're *all* connected!"

Liyana whispered to Poppy, "Who do they think he is?"

Poppy whispered back, "Who knows? Maybe they think he's our next-door neighbor from St.

Louis, since he's only speaking English. I just said he was our friend."

Omer, Khaled, and Nadine ate so much that everyone was complimented. The aunts always teased Liyana's family about living on "crumbs of bread and mint leaves." No one seemed suspicious of Omer, as Poppy had said they might. In fact, they seemed flattered that any mystery person would want to spend time with them. When you sat around with people, regular people with teacups and nutcrackers, they just wanted to get to know you.

Sitti threw her head back to gulp a soda straight from the bottle. A scraggly cat leapt through the doorway onto the ledge above Sitti's bed. She waved it away, muttering and mumbling.

"What's she saying?"

"I won't even begin to tell you." Poppy sighed.

Khaled said, "She told him he is not invited and he can go cook his own dinner with the other cats on the roof."

They ate and ate and ate. The whole day tasted wonderful. Afterward, when matches were struck for the awful after-dinner cigarettes and steam rose in small clouds from coffee cups, Omer said something directly to Sitti in slow, broken Arabic, which made the whole room go quiet. Now they *knew* he wasn't from St. Louis. A little hush rolled around the room.

Sitti replied in a voice more booming and animated than usual. It made Poppy sit straight up. Liyana tugged at him. "What is she saying?"

Everyone in the room pinned their eyes to her face. Except for Abu Daoud, who stormed from the room looking angry, after blurting something sharp to Omer. "What happened?" Liyana pulled Poppy's sleeve.

Poppy spoke haltingly. He didn't like translating if the person who had spoken could understand him. But sometimes he had to. Omer had said how much it meant to be with them. He thanked them for their welcome and said they felt like family to him. He wished they didn't have all these troubles in their shared country. Sitti said, "We have been waiting for you a very long time." But Abu Daoud, who now realized Omer's identity, hissed, "Remember us when you join your army."

———

Later Liyana would try to remember exactly what the room looked like during the next few moments. Maybe the light changed. Maybe the sunbeams falling across Sitti's bed intensified, and the small golden coffee pot glittered on its tray. The day turned a corner right then, but you would have to have been paying close attention to see it.

Sitti plunged into a new story, her voice dipping and swooping energetically, hands fluttering around her face. Omer stared at her with complete attention. Poppy frowned as she spoke.

"She's saying," Poppy translated hesitantly, as if the story tasted slightly bad in his mouth, "that your friend here reminds her very much—of someone she used to know. Someone—she liked a lot. Nobody knew it, though. He played a little flute—called a *nai*—that used to be more popular over here. This was—forty, fifty years ago? He was a shepherd and—he slept in a cave. Shepherds do that. Or, they used to."

"Cool!" Rafik said.

"And she was—married for a long time already. So she kept her feeling for him—hidden. For years. Maybe I shouldn't be telling you this! Maybe she shouldn't be telling me! Hmmmmm. She says—he 'saved her heart.'"

Poppy put his hand to his forehead and pinched it, massaging the skin the way he sometimes did when he was trying to work out a problem. But Sitti kept talking. Khaled and Nadine looked mesmerized. Liyana's cousins' mouths hung wide open. Aunt Saba let a cigarette burn down to a stump between her fingers and flicked it into the air when it stung her.

Poppy cleared his throat loudly and continued translating. "The shepherd—had a healing power, she says. For *air!* He could make the air feel calm again when it felt troubled. You know—after something bad happens—it's like a bad note hangs in the air? Hmmm—She says he could fix it. He would walk up a road—playing his flute. His flute—fixed it. I wish he were still here!"

Liyana's mother said, "Where is he now?"

Poppy held up one hand. "Wait a minute, she's going *on and on.* She says—your friend—has her friend's—same kind of hair. He has—his exact same shape of head. He has—something in the way he turns his eyes to things."

Now Sitti opened both her hands to Omer and said, *"Khallas."* Finished. The story was done—for the moment. She also said *"Shookran,"* thanking him, and smiling widely.

Omer leaned forward to take both her hands in his and thanked her back, in Arabic. The room stayed entirely quiet. Sitti laughed her gutsy, throaty laugh.

Poppy said, "She thinks your friend is—the angel—of her friend, who was killed in the '67 war. He wasn't fighting either. He was standing in front of a fruit shop in Nablus."

"You mean—she thinks Omer is his reincarnation?"

Poppy didn't know the word in Arabic, but he tried. She shook her head. "No, she says, *the angel.* I can't explain. She thinks one person can carry the spirit of another person in—an angel kind of way. Omer, you've got a load on your back you didn't even know about!"

Omer spoke softly. "I'm happy to carry him."

Omer and Liyana slipped away for another walk before sunset without Rafik or anyone else. Liyana felt sneaky, but relieved to have a few moments alone. If Sitti could be a renegade, then she could, too. They climbed the highest hill above the village to the abandoned stone house where her uncle used to live. He had been a recluse and almost never came down.

The path rose at a steep angle. Omer offered Liyana his hand more than once. When they were out of sight of the village, he no longer let hers go.

Weeds had grown up tall around the house's pale sunbaked stones. A cool breeze drifted through her uncle's open windows. He had died five years ago.

"What did he eat?" Omer asked.

"What he grew in his fields. They say he was very thin."

Inside the vacant house, they took deep breaths.

Liyana said, "My grandmother is full of surprises."

Omer said, "Oh Liyana. I'm glad your grandmother isn't mad that I came."

"Hardly!"

Liyana's throat flickered. She gulped and stared at him hard.

Omer said, "Do you think I kissed other people before? Well, I didn't. It's a big surprise to me. I don't want you to get in any trouble," he said. He kissed her hand.

She laughed. "Maybe a *little* trouble. I can't see any way around it." She leaned forward and kissed him one time on the mouth, then they both looked out the window into the valley, side by side.

Liyana did not think her uncle's spirit was angry with them for being on his hill. Distant plowed fields seemed to steam and breathe. She felt a great peacefulness floating in the air.

Poppy was standing outside looking up into the night sky when they appeared in the dark. He shook his finger at Liyana. But she knew sometimes he just pretended to be mad because he thought he ought to be. "Where have you been?"

"On the hermit tour."

Rafik and Nadine were collecting the popped bodies of balloons from the ground and handing them to Sitti, who stretched out the elastic skins and let them spring back to flatness. She groaned and looked entranced. Then she poked them into her belt.

Omer took both Sitti's hands in his again when they said good-bye. She peered deeply into his eyes and said, "Be careful! Come back! Please come back!"

Omer said, "Thank you, thank you, I am so happy to know you."

Liyana didn't even need translations.

On the drive home, Liyana felt exhausted in a good, full way. Rafik had hurt his knee on a rock and kept moaning in the back seat. Khaled said, "Now you're like me." The two of them were eating a handful of pumpkin seeds, pitching the shells out the open window into the blackness. Some of them flew back in and hit Liyana on the forehead. Normally she would complain. But this night she didn't care. She just brushed them away and leaned in Omer's direction.

Poppy said, "Today was quite an experience. Nineteen people asked me if they could borrow money."

Liyana's mother said she'd had the best day *ever* in the village and had finally learned how to make *lebne* by straining yogurt through cheesecloth. She thanked Khaled, Nadine, and Omer for their kindness to the children. "I don't think they will forget those balloons for a very long time." Poppy said he would drop Khaled and Nadine at the camp and drive Omer home since it was too late to catch a bus. Liyana could come along for the ride if she wanted to.

The roads were deserted at this hour. A skinny moon lay tipped on its back.

MAP

The calendar has a wide-open face.

Liyana lit one short candle in a blue glass cup and set it on the rug in front of her in her bedroom. Then she sat cross-legged before it. Everyone in her family had gone to sleep.

Flipping open an old notebook she'd written in just before she left St. Louis, she read, *It is hard to find anyone else who will admit they do not want to grow up. My friends say they're ready. Claire says it sounds great to her. Mom says she felt relieved to get older, even though she loved Peachy. Finally she was under "her own jurisdiction." That makes it sound like a court case. Poppy liked growing up because it meant he could travel "beyond the horizon." That makes it sound like "Over the Rainbow." Why does everything sound like something else?*

I want a map that says, "Here is the country of littleness, where words first fell into your mouths. Here are roads leading every direction. Some people will travel many roads. Some will set up camp close to their first homes. Some will stop loving their early words. Nothing will be enough for them. Keep your hearts simple and smooth

The entry ended there, in midair, without punctuation, after a sketch of a circle with squiggly lines extending out from it. Sometimes Liyana felt tempted to draw a large X over the pages in her notebooks.

Tonight she sat a long time before writing on the first page of one of the new blue notebooks Poppy had given her for her birthday. *There is no map.* She closed her eyes and waited. Then she wrote, *Every day is a new map. But it's just a scrap of it, an inch.*

Then she leaned back against her bed. *I like inches,* she wrote. *They're small enough to hold.*

The candle flame was swallowing itself. She tipped the glass to the side so the hot wax wouldn't smother the wick. In the other rooms of the house her parents and Rafik were wrapped in their deepest, dreamiest breaths by now. She stood, stretched, and stared out the window into the utterly clear night. A few tiny lights blinked from poles to the west and the south. People she would never know were sleeping in their beds and turning over.

An odd thought came to Liyana. Maybe this close feeling was a gift for growing older. Maybe this was what you got in place of all the things you lost.

How did a friend change your heart? Could

things still be simple? She didn't need *everyone* to know her—just a few people. That was enough. She needed her family, two countries, her senses, her notebooks and pencils, and her new devotion to—trade. When you liked somebody, you wanted to trade the best things you knew about. You liked them not only for themselves, but for the parts of you that they brought out.

It wasn't the beginning or end of any story, but the middle of—what felt rich.

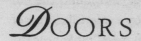

DOORS

There was a door in the heart
that had no lock on it.

Sitti wanted to show Omer her vineyard. She wanted him to tell her why her grapevines had dried up. Angels knew everything. She wanted to show him the treasures in her treasure box—the folded velvets and broken watches and golden buttons. She wanted him to travel with her to the Sea of Galilee.

"Why him?" Poppy asked. "Why don't you want to go alone with me?"

"Because he can speak Hebrew and you can't. And we may need it."

It was so rare for Sitti to leave the village. She wouldn't go to the Turkish baths in Nablus. She'd even decided to postpone her trip to Mecca again.

But she'd been having a craving for the little crispy fish that were caught and served at Galilee.

"No elevators," she said, shaking her finger at Poppy.

Rafik asked how she felt about boats.

"No boats!"

268   *Naomi Shihab Nye*

When they got to Galilee and found the old pink restaurant surrounded by a colorful clutter of buildings, they chose a green metal table near the water. Liyana's mother spoke to a waiter in Arabic even before they sat down, ordering water without ice for herself and hot tea for everyone else. Rafik ripped open a packet of crackers he had in his pocket and tossed them to three brown ducks who paddled up. He leaned over to feel the water.

"Yikes! It's cold. Sitti!" he said. "Let's go swimming!"

Liyana and Poppy pulled up an extra table so they would have enough room. The seaside breeze felt firm and cool. Sitti held her open hands toward the small waves as if she could push them back. She mumbled something. Poppy conveyed, "She's blessing—the energy. But she is also saying, Rafik, stay away from me!"

Reading the menu, Poppy said, "What do you know?" and shook his head. "The tourist industry has found this place! Too bad. It used to be so quiet and tucked away. Now the meals have biblical names."

They all ordered the same thing: *Disciple's Special.* A holy, purified meal. A picture on the menu showed crispy fish, moons of lemon, mounds of rice.

They drank their hot tea before the food came,

toasting the sea. Sitti gathered the empty teacups in front of her so she could read the grounds.

She waggled her finger at Rafik and yakked excitedly. Poppy sighed, "She says you need to study harder."

Liyana said, "I could have told you that without a teacup." Rafik lightly kicked her shin.

Next Sitti gazed into Omer's eyes, then his cup. She spoke in a deeper voice. Poppy translated, "You will need to be brave. There are hard days coming. There are hard words waiting in people's mouths to be spoken. There are walls. You can't break them. Just find doors in them. See?" Sitti's white scarf lifted in the breeze. "You already have. Here we are, together."

Omer said, "All that in my tea leaves? They're very talkative!" He smiled at Sitti.

Liyana's mother put her arm around Poppy and pulled his chair closer to hers. The sun was glistening on her head like a spotlight.

Sitti tapped the rim of Liyana's cup, tipping it back and forth.

"I think she's cheating!" Rafik said. "She's moving your leaves around so they say something better! Have you ever noticed how my cup is always bossy and your cup always holds a compliment?" He threw a hand to his forehead and Omer laughed.

Sure enough, Sitti said the leaves in the bottom of Liyana's cup promised her a beautiful future.

"Revolting," muttered Rafik.

"Walk and talk," Poppy translated. "Walk and talk." He tipped his head and winked.

"She knows your specialties, anyway," Omer whispered.

Sitti touched her first two fingers to Liyana's forehead, and crooned. Poppy said, "She says you have a powerful world in there. Be strong. Keep letting it out."

Liyana looked down at her own hands folded on the table and said, very softly, "I'll try."

Their full plates were arriving. Sitti took a ravenous nibble before everyone else was served. She kissed her fingers. Another waiter collected the cups. Poppy sliced. He sliced and sliced. Was it tough? He took a tentative bite, beckoned to the first waiter, and pointed sadly at his fish. "I'm sorry," he said, his face crinkling good-naturedly, "but it's not *quite*—delicious."